4

33525

Dare to Dream

Pádraig Òe Rís

authorHOUSE®

AuthorHouse™ UK Ltd.
500 Avebury Boulevard
Central Milton Keynes, MK9 2BE
www.authorhouse.co.uk
Phone: 08001974150

First published by AuthorHouse 11/10/2009

ISBN: 978-1-4490-4624-8 (sc)

This book is printed on acid-free paper.

Prefix

A brief history of the Industrial Schools system in
Ireland

1868. The Industrial Schools Act. Industrial
Schools were established to care for
neglected, orphaned and abandoned
children. They were run by religious orders
and funded by public funds.

1924. The new Irish State's Department of
Education noted that there were more
children in Industrial schools in the Irish
Free State than in the whole of the United
Kingdom.

1929. The Children's Act allowed for destitute
children to be sent to Industrial Schools
without having committed a crime.

1933. Industrial schools were abolished in the UK
but were retained in Ireland.

1934. The (Judge) Cussen report expressed
reservations about the large number of
children in 'care', the inadequate nature
of their education and stigma attached to

the schools. Yet it still recommended they stay under the management of religious orders.

1943. St. Joseph's in County Cavan, run by the Nuns Order of Poor Clares, burnt to the ground killing 35 girls and an elderly woman. The Nuns were exonerated in the enquiry.

1944. P. O'Muircheartaigh, Inspector of Schools, reported "The children are not properly fed there is semi-starvation and the lack of care and attention."

1945. Secretary to the Department of Education wrote to the Secretary of the Department of Finance to denounce the grave situation that had arisen regarding the feeding and clothing of children in Industrial Schools due to parsimony and criminal negligence.

1946. Father Flanagan, founder of Boys Town schools for orphans and delinquents in the United States visited Irish Industrial Schools and described them as a national disgrace. This led to a public debate in Government and the media. State and Church pressure forced him to leave Ireland. He died of a heart attack in 1948, as did the debate on Industrial Schools.

1951. State Inspector denounced conditions in the schools and the care of the children.

1954. Government debate on Michael Flanagan, whose arm was broken while in care at Artane Industrial School, the case was dismissed as "an isolated incident".

1955. The Secretary of State for the Department of Education visited Daingean Industrial School in County Offaly and found the cows were better fed than the boys. No action was taken for another 16 years

1963. The Bundoran Incident. Eight girls trying to escape from St. Martha's Industrial School had their heads shaved. It became a scandal when it was front-page news in a British tabloid press with photos and headline; "Orphanage Horror". A Department of Education official visited the Mother Superior of the School to tell her "The Department was unlikely to do anything of a disciplinary nature".

1967. The Department of Health visits Ferryhouse Industrial School in Clonmel to investigate the death of a child from meningitis. They described the conditions as "a social malaise" and recommended the closure of the school.

1969. The notorious Artane Industrial School was closed.

1970. The District Justice Eileen Kennedy's report for the Department of Justice which was established to examine Industrial Schools, recommended that they be closed. The Justice was appalled by the Dickensian and deplorable state of the schools. The report revealed that many case histories showed that the schools were training grounds for youthful offenders. It acknowledged that all children need love, care and security if they are to develop. Children in the institutions have, for the most part, been deprived of this attention.

The Kennedy Committee visited Daingean School in 1968 where the manager Father McGonagle, told them 'without embarrassment' about how the children were stripped naked to be strapped on the buttocks. A Department of Justice Official present reported that the Father said, "he considered punishment to be more humiliating when children were stripped naked for it". The account produced shockwaves in the Department of Justice. Secretary Peter Berry, writing to his opposite number in the Department of Education described such practices as "indefensible", adding that if it became known it would "cause a grave public scandal". It never did become known at the time, though the Kennedy Committee recommended the school's immediate closure.

1976. RTE (Irish Broadcasting Service) broadcast pays tribute to Brother Joseph O'Connor, founder of the Artane Boys Band. He was subsequently proved to be a multiple rapist of boys at Artane School.

1998. The Christian Brothers make a public apology to those children who were physically or sexually abused.

1999 Irish Prime Minister Bertie Ahern makes a public apology to victims.

THE BATTERY CHILDREN

Self-preservation is one of our prime instincts and I believe the brain has an inbuilt coping mechanism which provides that protection. For most of my life it has served me well. Memories that should have been my childhood, I chose to seal away in the dark recesses of my mind. Shame and fear prevented me from questioning the circumstances that left me bereft of a family background.

It was only in early 2006 that I summoned up the courage to uncover some of the reasons why I had spent the whole of what should have been my childhood in Industrial Schools.

Under the Irish Freedom of Information Act, the only information the government provided, revealed that I had appeared at Dublin District Court as a two year old. There, on 10th February 1934, I was charged with receiving alms and sentenced as young juvenile by Judge Cussen to be detained in Industrial Schools until my 16th birthday and assigned a number - 11536. For the next 14 years I served my time in two of these schools. Firstly at St. Patrick's for boys in County Kilkenny, until at age ten I was considered a young adult and transferred to Artane Industrial School in County Dublin to start my working life.

It was only at my 'final disposal' at age 16 that

I discovered, too late, that I had blood relatives. Within a matter of weeks I had severed all contact with these newly found relatives with the exception of one sister whom I tracked down before leaving Ireland at age 17.

My first eight years of 'corrective training' were served at St. Patrick's Industrial School in County Kilkenny, where most of the children were either orphaned or abandoned. Too young to know any different, I now consider myself fortunate to have avoided the painful emotional experience of many other children. Older boys were wrenched away in spite of tearful frenzied protests of a Mother, herself often a widow, to be handed over to Institutions by Irish Authorities. The Institutions were paid three times the amount received by a widow in the form of her pension. If she had been paid the same amount, she could have kept her child in comfort.

The Church preached the sacredness of the family, and yet there was no voice to be heard against the interference of the State with the rights of the parent. The Church commended it; the State could do no wrong when it served the wishes of the priests and bishops. The Catholic Church and the state were one and the same. The rulers and the well off hastened their children off to boarding school, seeing them only during holidays. Only when their children came of an age to be able to engage in intelligent conversation, did they associate with them. Having attended public and private schools made them very important people. It should therefore come as no surprise that their mind set towards 'unfortunate' children, was to do as I have done, say as I have said, think as I do, read what I have read. Follow your leader, it was a perpetual example.

To my mind my life started at St. Patrick's, surrounded by other children, where Nuns of the Sisters of Charity were in charge. As birthdays were of no significance, our starting in school classes meant we had reached around five years old, and our first communion signalled we had reached the 'age of reason', seven years old. Suddenly, one day, I was informed that I was a young man of ten and that it was time to move on. At the time I was unaware of my date of birth, but the record shows that I was a month passed my tenth birthday. As a lone young man I was transferred back to Dublin to serve out my remaining six years in Artane. There, my working life started in the machine shop, making and repairing clothing, darning holed socks and finishing off new machine made stockings by knitting up the ends. For my final trade assignment I was employed on the poultry farm.

Of the 800 boys at the school, I was one of the few 'Nobodies', orphans and unwanted children who had been abandoned by family members. The fortunate inmates whose relatives visited on a monthly basis were also released to family members for the summer holidays, Christmas, Easter and other vacations throughout the year. The 'Nobodies' were required to carry on with the care and upkeep of the poultry, the livestock on the farm, the garden produce and crops.

A private report on Artane Industrial School by a Father Henry Moore to the Most Reverent John C. McQuaid, D. D. Lord Archbishop of Dublin, Primate of Ireland, in July 1962 differs little from the description I outlined in the story 'Lonesome Stray', of life as I knew it in Artane from 1941 to 1947. My understanding is that his report was kept secret for some 45 years. My reaction on reading it for the first time in March 2008 was to find his perceptions, views, and his recommendations very amusing and I will tell you why. Of course my view of the report is a retrospective one, due to the long lapse of time.

He starts the report by discussing the management of the school, writing that "the methods are obsolete, proper training is neglected and there's no attempt to adequate rehabilitate." How does one rehabilitate a young beggar, who has already served eight years of his time prior to being transferred to Artane? He continues:

> "boys leaving Artane having already spent 10 to 14 years in an institutional environment, it's readily acknowledged that they require specialized treatment. A fundamental defect is in the admission system, the indiscriminate manner they are admitted, without regard to background, medical history, antecedents or suitability for the training they receive. The atmosphere is

unreal in regards to the lack of contact with the opposite sex. This unnatural situation among hundreds of boys and staff leads to a degree of sexual maladjustment in the boys."

As a priest he appeared well versed in sexual matters, yet he failed to recommend adding sex education to the curriculum. I think it can be proven without doubt that, in later years, a high degree of sexual maladjustment already existed in some of the Christian Brothers throughout Ireland. "The boys were denied the opportunity to develop normally. When liberated their reactions were often violent and irresponsible." It wouldn't do to encourage the boys to see, hear, think, and reason for themselves, so as to do for themselves. Sadly at three score and ten years of age, many of us are still frightened children. The foundations of nurturing and love were never afforded the child. The good priest failed to take on board how well trained we were, a word he keeps repeating. This is well demonstrated by our reaction to the command of the whistle, to come to attention, to sit, to eat, to run, plus we could spout English and Latin words like a parrot, without having a clue as to their meaning.

While I'm willing to accept his well-meaning comments, I can now see why nothing changed in the intervening 15 years since my final disposal in 1947. Reports as far back as 1934 were not acted upon. To have introduced change would have meant giving up a degree of control. Had the children, as he refers to them, been given the opportunity to develop normally, helped to learn, how did he envisage the children would react?

Considering the facts in his report as a whole, I can well envisage, with our superior strength in numbers, 800 boys to 20 Brothers, we could well have overpowered our tormentors and taken control of what we viewed as prison. Freedom gained cannot be bottled. The result of such an uprising may well have brought about an earlier demise of the Industrial Schools system, or greater discipline as the little buggers demonstrate their delinquency for all to see.

He went on to outline diet essentials stating: "that butter and fruit are never used." I'm still left wondering what happened with all the fruit from the garden, the meat, eggs and other produce from the farms and poultry farm; not to feed the children I can vouch. He continues; "in general the boys are undernourished, lacking in calcium and other components. In addition to the three daily meals there is a light refreshment of a slice of bread and jam"! Well things must have improved with the introduction of jam after 1947, my disposal year. Although he is not best pleased with the manner it is transported to the 'yard' (parade ground). Neither is he impressed by the method of its service, "in a large sized wooden box, the boys are paraded to receive their portion, it's crude and unhealthy."

His observations are of our "unruly

indelicate manner at the refectory table." What did he expect of us? Obedience came high on the training schedule, not to educate, but to control our every move, hence the animal behaviour.

Later in the report, he turned to discussing our dress: "This aspect of care is grossly neglected." He states the clothing is "uncomfortable, unhygienic and of a displeasing sameness. Both boys and clothing are dirty. The material is poor because it's manufactured on the premises." Oh dear, that is not very kind of him, that's our 'school uniform' he's denigrating, plus we are self-sufficient when it comes to making and repairing our clothing. Had he visited the latrines he might have better understood the conditions, plus the reasons our clothes and us were dirty.

He had also learnt that overcoats "are only for the boys who can afford to buy them." The boys whose parents visited them, in addition to providing food parcels, passed on what little money they could afford to part with. In my final year I managed to avail myself of a much sought after overcoat, for the princely sum of £1 and ten shillings. This was money I had obtained by selling the Brothers' white bread and other delicacies won from the refuse collection from their dining tables, to the more affluent inmates. Part of my duties was the daily collection of refuse for delivery to the poultry farm for use in feeding the livestock.

The sight of hundreds of boys walking the roads in file on Sundays, in the deep of winter without overcoats, he found pathetic. This ritual did not apply to boys over 14 years old. By then they were in full unpaid employment in their given trade. My choice to work on the poultry farm was motivated by hunger: I wished to share in the well-fed lifestyle of the livestock.

He remarks, "There's no such thing as personal property when it comes to clothing, except for owners of overcoats." The new clothing and shoes I was provided with by the Nuns on my departure from St. Patrick's vanished soon after my arrival at Artane. Stealing my only possessions was not very Christian. Robbed of my only worldly possessions they were replaced with clothing and footwear that belonged to no one, but had been passed on for years from inmates past and present. The only possessions I was left with were my name, Charlie and number, 11536. By the time I was due for disposal I would even lose my name.

Father Moore continued: "Stockings, footwear and nightshirts are handed down from generations, no pyjamas." Should anyone have questioned me about pyjamas, my response may well have been "what are they?" His report notes that the same hobnailed boots and clothing are worn all year round, summer and winter. At the weekly change of clothing it was first come, first grab - survival of the fittest - and the aim was to find clothing with as few patches as possible and hope for a fair fit. He observed, "There are no handkerchiefs." Our coat sleeves conveniently served to wipe nose, mouth and tear-stained eyes.

To substitute this service with a handkerchief would have been unlikely to succeed. I could envisage a hankie being utilised to hold the collection of hobnails, steel tips and the U shaped heel pieces from the soles of boots that were gathered from about the parade ground. A kiosk located in the play hall and managed by a Brother sold small portions of cheese for a few pence in exchange for a collection of metal. A hankie would have provided useful wrapping for such a rare delicacy as cheese, instead of loose in our pockets with jack-stones and our other bits and pieces.

Describing the medical set up, he explained: "There is no nurse or matron in attendance. A Brother without medical qualifications was transferred from the care of the poultry farm, to be in charge of all medical arrangements. The surgery next to the 'dining hall' resembles a vacated dairy house." Having worked on the poultry farm for two years, I can vouch that by comparison with our conditions, the livestock were free, well-fed, watered, well cared for and the houses cleaned daily.

He noted that some boys suffered from enuresis and were left untreated. I fear his diagnosis was flawed. The smell of urine was prevalent due to the training methods employed. These induced fear, by daily beating the different subjects into the boys resulting, not surprisingly, in many boys wetting themselves.

Writing about discipline, he reports: "Every activity is marshalled, even the recitation of the

Angelus during recreation. A regular beating breeds undue fear and anxiety." Why did he think some suffered from enuresis? "Their liberty is so restricted that all initiative and self esteem suffers. The personality is repressed, maladjusted and in some cases abnormal. They find it difficult to establish ordinary human relationships."

As an inmate I cannot recall ever being treated as an ordinary human. Abnormal 'teaching' methods resulted in abnormal behaviour in the boys. The fear of beatings served to keep the inmates under tight control. The report continues: children who had no visitors, nor family to take them on home visits - the ones I referred to as 'Nobodies' in 'Lonesome Stray' - were transferred to work on the farms during holiday periods. "This breeds discontent and frustration". On the contrary I, and many like me, knew no different and suffered no ill effects. The work proved to be better and safer than confinement in a classroom, where the teaching methods I would liken to training a parrot. Only we received the strap in the hope of producing the required response.

When referring to the School Band, Father Moore felt obliged to refer to a "Protestant Layman who's constant practice was to accompany the boys on each and every engagement. It is my opinion the man renders no service to the school and should not be present." When he questioned the Brother concerning the Protestant Layman: "I found him not only discourteous but impertinent." At least I find this very amusing, what kind of men did he think were required to maintain control over these unruly inmates? A Layman would provide a good front for the band on their engagements. Should any boy be so stupid as to dare to question a 'Brother' without first being addressed, he could expect to be thrashed within an inch of his life.

I concur with his statement that "many 'ex-pupils' find the practice of their Faith a burden to be shunned as they associate their religious training with repression." Training there was, learning to understand was non-existent. "Too often Christian Doctrine classes were without enthusiasm, and lacking incentive." He repudiates the use of physical punishment for failure at these lessons. "At times it's excessive!" Sure he failed to understand, they were trying to beat the message of the Doctrine into us. They knew no different and neither did we. Too afraid to question the meaning of sins, we wondered; how does one covet a neighbour's wife? Or for that matter how does one commit adultery? I have no doubt such questions would have been met with a severe beating, leaving the child confused and wondering what tree might be considered a dull tree.

Father Moore relates how he received letters from ex-pupils and was amazed by their illegible form and unintelligible content. Of 22 boys aged ranging from 10 to 14, only seven could write with assistance. In view of the training they received it shouldn't have come as any surprise to him. The strap was the normal 'assistance'.

"Boys are allotted various trades without

reference to their suitability or preference. A factual proof of this is the way the boys are placed on leaving School." In my case the only factual proof, presented to me for the first time in 2006 under the Freedom of Information Act, reads:

- "Number in General Register: 75462.
- Name and Number in Industrial School: Patrick Charles Rice, 11536.
- Date of Birth: 8 October 1931.
- When, where and by who ordered to be detained: Dublin DC Judge Cussen, 10 February 1934.
- With what charged: Receiving Alms.
- Date of discharge: 7 October 1947.
- Payment per week: Nil.
- Ultimate Disposal: to his Mother, 4 Florence Street, South Circular Road, Dublin. For employment at Western Hotel, South Circular Road as a page boy for ten shillings a week (in today's currency equal to 50 pence or about 30 US cents).

It appears that the official records are not worth the paper they are recorded on. The only period I would have lived with this 'Mother' could have been from birth to the date of my incarceration as a two year old. During my incarceration I was unaware that I had any relatives. Not until I was due for disposal at 16 did I discover for the first time that I had a Mother and a sister. The sister decided that I was to live with her on my release.

I'm amazed that anyone would believe that a child, who had been locked away from the outside world, could even be considered for a position as a page boy in a hotel. Having worked unpaid on a poultry farm for the preceding two years was hardly ideal preparation for work in a hotel, even for ten shillings a week. Father Moore's report continues: "Of 140 boys disposed of in two years 75% were placed in employment for which they were never trained. In the five years prior to the report 80% of the boys emigrated and lapsed entirely from the faith." Count me as one of those.

He concludes: "I strongly recommend the introduction of female personnel, preferably Nuns, who would take care of the domestic arrangements and charge of the small boys." To even consider this recommendation had any merit, I submit he must have been living in La La land. If he found the reaction of the Brother in charge of the band "not only discourteous but impertinent" when he referred to the Protestant Layman having no service to the school, the Brothers' reaction to the arrival of Nuns at the school leaves much to the imagination. Had he been more forward thinking, he might well have suggested the introduction of sex education for the inmates, or should it be 'training', the word he prefers. Then again maybe not, sex is something Sisters and Brothers don't indulge in, I'm sure that is why they are called a 'none'.

Having digested the contents of this report

it comes as no surprise that it was kept secret for 45 years. Irish Society might at the time have been best served had the assignment to report on Artane Industrial School been allocated to a well-qualified woman psychologist. Even then it is doubtful that such a report would have been acted upon in view of the lack of action on Father Henry Moore's report, and other reports down through the years before him. To this day religious orders are still in denial regarding the damage they inflicted on individuals, their families and society as a whole. Many appear unable to recognise any failings. Not unlike the man who remarked to the butcher: "How much is the sheep's head in the window?" "That's not a window, it's a mirror," replied the butcher.

Many of their charges on disposal were unprepared for life in the outside world. From my own experience and those of others, it would be accurate to assume that after the years of 'training' they ended up as misfits, psychologically flawed, dysfunctional, emotionally barren and uneducated in the ways of the world. Many may well have gone on to produce dysfunctional families.

The one conclusion I've reached when I reflect on the years spent in state custody is that there is no way I should look up to these men as an example but rather as a warning.

My sentence completed, it was decided that following my disposal from Artane I should be returned to the custody of the woman from whom I had been removed fourteen years earlier. For reasons unknown to me she in turn handed the custody over to my new newly married twenty year old sister. In 2006, for the first time I read the date of my disposal: 7th October 1947. The significance of the date in 1947 went unnoticed due to my ignorance of my actual date of birth. Birthdays went unnoticed during my 14 years served in institutions. The strangers into whose custody I had been entrusted, nominally a Mother and sister, failed to mention the word birthday on the following day when I turned 16. No explanation was asked or given, as to why these women never visited me during the long years of my incarceration. It was as if they had come to pick up a stray from a dog pound and the dog was not wagging its tail for its new owners. Still I was pleased to be away from the cursed school on a cold gray October day with a sky deeper and heavier gray hanging down overhead. No comfort without but joy within, I was getting away from a place that was a menace to health and daily life. I had never attempted to escape: too scared of the consequences. The institution taught a damaging docility. What a time I had, never free for a second, always under discipline, forever watched.

The women into whose custody I found myself were ill-equipped to re-train this overgrown child in the ways of a strange new world. For my part there were no feelings of any kind towards these women, they were just strangers. I had more in common with the boys I had grown up with.

Sharing one room in a tenement building with a strange young sister Margaret, and her husband, could only last until I discovered a new sense of freedom. No longer did I have to remain with anyone or in any one place. With the threat of physical punishment for failing to obey commands removed, I could no longer be hurt. No longer restrained I was free to come and go as I pleased. As a lone stray young lad, I took any offer and moved on without a thank you or a good bye. There had been no one in my life except for the faceless sea of boys, Nuns and Christian Brothers.

To survive in this new world I would forever have to be on my guard, everyone is a stranger. Only by looking and listening could I attempt to mimic acceptable social behaviour. Restless with this new found freedom I roamed Dublin city like a stray dog seeking food, shelter, and work. Following my natural instincts I kept on the move from job to job, four in five months with three different places to lay my head. At the final boarding house I met other young men who had spent a period of their childhood in the Industrial School system. Like them I unknowingly found what I had been looking for, a home from home, the armed forces.

Some relationships I could not, nor would ever experience. I could only observe. The shared love of a Mother and child, Father and child, what does it feel like for a child in the warm safe embrace of a parent? How does a child feel, running free around a playground at school laughing and screaming, and at the end of the day to go HOME? Why do grown-ups hug one another? I only hugged my children and grandchildren until they reached an age to make a free choice to hug, or be hugged. I have savoured the joys in observing the excitement of our children and grandchildren opening birthday and Christmas presents. These kinds of experiences were non-existent in my childhood and young adulthood.

It is therefore all the more surprising that the girl I first felt drawn to from across a dance hall floor should later accept my proposal of marriage. Though I was unaware of it then, here I was a psychologically flawed, dysfunctional, emotionally barren and social misfit, asking a beautiful young factory girl to marry him. In fairness I did warn her that I was just a stray with no family and all I had to offer was my heart bursting with love. Once she accepted my proposal I became whole and with the passing of each day I fell deeper and deeper in love. There are two sentences she would repeat often over the years: "You're strange" and "Please don't show me up". For a young girl who grew up in a coal mining village in County Durham, and started work in a clothing factory at 14, our marriage must have turned out to be a real roller coaster ride for her. Uneducated and with some handicaps in my make up, the power of her unconditional and inspirational love, was the driving force behind my efforts to achieve promised dreams. Though I did not know it then, not only had I found a wife, but subconsciously I had gained a Mom.

If my childhood could be considered tragic, it was as nought compared with the experiences we would share over a long and loving relationship. By any standards we lived a full life and through it all, the power of love provided me with the determination and inspiration to go where, but a few might attempt to go.

Early in our marriage I accompanied my wife on a visit to Artane intent on her seeing for herself the place I had spent six of my formative years. During our visit we came across a young lad who was returning from a day visit with his parents. To every question asked, he sprang to attention with a yes sir, or no sir, waiting to be told he might carry on. My wife proclaimed that she had never met such a good mannered young boy before. That was me in earlier years I pointed out.

In the documents released to me under the Irish Freedom of Information Act, it appears the follow-up after my Ultimate Disposal was non-existent. Had there been a proper follow-up it would have revealed that I had not lived with the woman to whom I was introduced to as my 'Mother'. One would think a hotel employer would check out a 16 year old lad who had spent his previous 14 years locked away, before employing him. Recent records reveal I left the hotel, "because the work was too hard", I'd just spent two years working unpaid on the poultry farm, seven days a week, from early morning to late evening.

All other information is blanked out; "To protect other children's identity".

A TIME OF LEARNING

Our marriage was a most unlikely union. The overriding factor in our relationship was a deep enduring love and to say love is blind would be a true understatement of such a strange relationship. I am sure Jean had no idea or expectations about what she had entered into. This was truly a journey into the unknown for both of us. On reflection it must have been a very scary period in her life, taking on a husband who knew next to nothing about relationships or social behaviour.

A married quarter at an RAF Base in Lincolnshire was to be our very first home. Words fail to describe my feeling when entering the front door of that house. Here we were starting out on a life together a long way from whence we had come. Jean had never lived away from her family in Co. Durham, whilst I had come from Ireland where my formative years were spent locked away in Institutions.

Though the pay was poor we did have security and as a Corporal I was better off than other lower ranked young married men starting out. It proved exciting to love, to have a home and to experience the love of another human for the very first time in my life. More exciting was the joyful news that Jean was with child; we were to be a family. It was the start of a family for me. Sadly our children would only have grandparents and a large extended family on Jean's side. Nonetheless we had started our very own family.

Life was perfect, but then came the first of many disruptions that form part of Service life. I was to be posted to a unit in the Shetlands Isles, to be precise the RAF unit of Saxa Vord which was located on the Isle of Unst, the most northerly of the isles. This was the worst kind of move, to a place where no married accommodation existed, which meant Jean had to return to her family in Co. Durham. I made my way by ship from Aberdeen and onwards overland by ferry and vehicle between small islands to my new Base.

During the following years in the Services, this posting stands out as one of the two worst places I've had the misfortune to serve. It was a small, bleak, wind-swept, rock-strewn Island. Due to the fierce westerly winds the vegetation was flattened, even the few existing trees that guarded the Island Doctor's house were stunted. The only animals suited to the terrain were sheep and Shetland Ponies, so there was no milk to be had. The sale or purchase of alcohol was prohibited on the Shetlands Isles, except for the one brand of beer delivered from Scotland for consumption within the confines of the base. Like all attempts to outlaw alcohol, it provided the opportunity for those willing to make a profit to fill the vacuum. The craving for something stronger than the available brand of beer was met, by buying or exchanging a bottle of beer for one of the illegally distilled Moonshine. The one redeeming factor to the place was that I neither liked the beer nor wished to waste money on the already limited supply of goods on sale at the local store. The store and post office were located at Haroldswick, some distance from our unit. It reminded me of something out of an old western movie with its low wooden construction that contained everything required for work and daily living, clothing, footwear and food. The warmest month of the year was August when the average temperature was 14 Celsius. On average it rained or showered 285 days a year. The weather conditions dictated the ferry's arrival and departure times with its delivery and dispatch of mail, supplies and personnel. As few houses possessed telephones during the 1950's, our only form of communication was by letter.

My first impression of the base was a very depressing one; a collection of low, flat-roofed Nissan huts each with tall wind-brushed radio antenna resting atop, like the odd strand of hair on a bald head. The unit was small enough to warrant just the one dining hall and kitchen with a small room set aside for the two officers. I don't remember any Senior Non-commissioned Officer being stationed on the unit, during my time there.

I can clearly recall my first weekend at the base. As we lay on our bunks after lunch, I asked what there was to do on weekends. The bored response was; "The canteen will be opening up later where there's a pool table and a bar to drink at. When it's dry and not too windy you can go for a walk and there's the radio to listen to. Three nights a week we have a film show." The latter I was aware of, as I'd been assigned to operate the projector. Just when my spirits sank to new depths, the door opened and the C.O, a RAF Squadron Leader and one of the two officers on the base, popped his head around the door; "How would you chaps like to go for a ride?" The excited men made a mad rush for the door; I tagged along in anticipation of an interesting afternoon's excitement. Well wrapped up against the weather we piled into a large four-wheel drive vehicle. The only other vehicle of its kind on the island was used by the naval officer. Off we traveled over the rough terrain to the foot of a hill by the shore's edge where we disembarked. We strode over the hill chatting as we went until signaled by the C.O to be quiet. On the hilltop he motioned us to be quiet, to lie flat and peer below to the sea where a number of Grey Seals were playing in the water. As I observed the enthusiasm etched on the faces of the C.O and the men, I thought; is this the best I can look forward to each weekend? But no there was more excitement to come. Making our way back to the vehicle over the bleak wind-swept terrain; we came upon a small stream. The lads settled down to play by the stream throwing rocks, while the C.O drove off on a foray of his own, leaving us to our 'fun'. As I watched the antics of these men I was minded of children at play. A number of them made tiny paper boats

27

only for others to try and sink them by throwing rocks. They were laughing and shouting, having a wonderful time. That evening in the canteen, I listened as the fellows told others who had been unfortunate in missing the afternoon's adventure of watching the seals and knocking one another's boats out of the water! My goodness, I feared for my sanity.

On 27th September 1956, I was summoned to the C.O's office: "Congratulations, this telegram states that you are the proud father of a baby boy!" I didn't know whether to cry or jump for joy. Jean had given birth to our child, of her own flesh and blood, our very own child! We had already agreed on names Seán (John) for a boy, and Colleen (term of endearment for a little girl). Our son would be the next generation of Jean's family and the start of a new generation of mine. From my side there would be no grandparents for our son but with the arrival of a child a fresh foundation to my life was laid. Starting a family gave real purpose to my life, the motivation to work hard towards my preconceived ideal of family life.

After some consideration I thought it best to wait and spend our first Christmas with our newborn. My application for leave was promptly approved. What better time of the year than Christmas to spend in the bosom of my new family at Jean's home. The weather held out that December, allowing for safe travel overland to the main island Lerwick and then onward by ship to Aberdeen. Often ferries were delayed for days

Jean with our first born, Seán

on end due to bad weather, as happened on my return to Base, when I was forced to stay over at a hotel for a number of days to await a break in the weather.

In the early months of the New Year news of a new posting came as a wonderful relief. The new assignment was in total contrast to any other unit I had served on until that point, or for that matter would serve at in the future. The change of location from the remote Shetland Isles to my new unit could not have been more different in every respect. The new location was a Movements Unit in Belgium; its function was to oversee the receipt and dispatch of military equipment at Antwerp

Docks to and from military units throughout Europe.

Like so many earlier journeys I made my lone way to the Hook of Holland by ship and onward by train to Antwerp. At the railway station I found a small office staffed by what looked like British soldiers. They turned out to be Belgium servicemen who kindly arranged transport to my new unit. The civilian driver I assumed to be of Belgium origin because of my problem understanding his English. On arrival at our destination in the middle of a busy street, I asked for the time and only then I did recognize his accent. He was a County Cork man! Answering me in a familiar sing song dialect "Tin te Tin", (ten to ten) there was no mistaking that same sounding voice of yore, Christian Brother 'Bocker' Murphy. A voice from my childhood that still stirred painful memories of the unmerciful beating I received about my necked body with the use of his leather strap.

The tall building that served as our Base housed all ranks with the exception of officers. The ground floor served as a reception/orderly room, not unlike a hotel reception desk, and located at the rear of the building were the other ranks' kitchen and dining room. The second floor housed the Sergeants' Mess and living quarters, while the other ranks' sleeping accommodation was located on the top floor. Officers and married personnel were assigned private rented accommodation in locations throughout the city. My duty would be to oversee the running of the Sergeants' mess bar and other ranks' mess hall.

It took two weeks to complete all the arrangements for my family to join me in our newly assigned apartment in the city. During this short period I noted that most of the men went to bed after their meal at around five o'clock. Then around ten o'clock it was time for them to get up and indulge in the city's nightlife. It seemed the city never slept, as the cafes/bars remained open around the clock. Many single men spent their off duty time in the different bars around the block in which our unit was located. Some never managed to complete the trip around the block, being a little the worst for wear when they returned to sleep it off before turning in for work the following morning.

Once we had settled into our apartment in Koraalberg we were able to invite Jean's Mum and her older sister with her two young girls to spend a vacation in Belgium with us. For our weekly night out we were in the habit of visiting a nearby café/bar run by what is now referred to as a 'gay' couple. Jean found she was always welcome there, the 'chaps' confided in her and she was always a good listener. To entertain Jean's Mum and sister, we took them to the heart of the city to watch a drag artist's show. This was a new world to them and I found it very amusing to see the look of sheer disbelief on her sister's face as she beckoned to her Mother: "Look at them two men, they're kissing!" It brought howls of laughter from her Mum.

Our stay in Antwerp was all too short and before long we were on the move again on to a new destination in Germany. The transfer to a new unit I suspected may well have been a move of connivance due to Jean's condition. The nearest suitable hospital for military personnel and families, that could manage births was located at a British Military Hospital in Germany. By then our son Seán, was a little more than a year old and Jean was expecting our second child. Though I didn't realise it at the time she already had two children on her hands as I was sharing in a new found childhood delight of mischief, fun and the wonder of seeing the world through the eyes of our child. To Jean's annoyance I had taught Seán that whenever she questioned his wrong doings he was to reply; "It wasn't me it was Mr Nobody."

Handorf, my new unit, was a small communications headquarters responsible for trailer units that were manned by a handful of men operating throughout West Germany. I reported to my new unit ahead of my family in order to prepare our new accommodation. The corporal in charge of the orderly room welcomed me with a mischievous grin as he directed me to the second-in-command's office; "Try not to look too surprised when you meet the Adjutant, he's waiting to see you."

The sign on the door read: Flight Lieutenant Russ, Adjutant. I was welcomed in: "Well hello there, and what do they call you?" "Corporal Rice sir" I replied. "No, no I mean what's your first name?" When I told him it was Patrick, he asked if it was OK to call me 'Paddy' to which I agreed. Leaning across his desk with hands folded, he spoke in a soft friendly voice; "Well now Paddy, as there are only two officers running this unit, the C.O and I. The Officers Mess is much too small to warrant employing a corporal. The job I have in mind for you is the management of the corporals' club and bar. I'm sure you will enjoy your stay here. Pop back and have a word with Corporal Montgomery who will fill you in on the details of the unit and its personnel."

From what I had seen and heard it appeared that the controlling power of the unit was in the hands of a number of gay personnel. The C.O, a Squadron Leader, was a pleasant easy-going chap nicknamed 'Dad' Aston, who was married and living off the Base. The Adjutant was referred to as 'Rusty' and among his gay friends there was a vehicle mechanic from the motor pool whom Rusty chose as his personal batman. The medical quarters was run by a Corporal Willis who swaggered about the place smoking from a long cigarette holder. At the bar in the evenings he wore brightly coloured clothing, primarily a collection of dazzling waistcoats. There appeared to be a good-humoured acceptance by the rest of the men of their gay colleagues. However, I recall a moment of unrest that occurred in the dining room one weekend when breakfast had not been prepared on time for the sudden influx of men. It appeared that 'Rusty' had arisen in a bad mood and decided to tear around the barracks rooms rousing the men from their beds, with a loud "Wakie wakie, rise and shine." A large number of men including the cooks arrived in the dining hall together and in the rush to prepare the meal, a difference of opinion arose between the senior cook and the friendly gay cooks, 'Cathy' and 'Mona'. The 'boys' were aptly named; Mona did tend to moan, whilst Cathy as the name implied was catty by nature. The row was still in full flow when 'Rusty' appeared on the scene. The problem was settled when Mike, the senior cook, was ordered to report to the officer's office later in the day. Later that evening in the bar I asked Corporal Mike why he looked so glum and was surprised when he told me: "I've been ordered to be outside the main gates by 17:00 hours this evening." It seemed he had been deemed a disruptive influence and like any others found to disrupt the harmony of the Base, he was moved on to one of the many remote trailer outposts.

Meanwhile our family had settled into our new accommodation some distance from the Base. Journeys to and from work and functions were made on the Base bus and there was an every ready supply of babysitters, which allowed us to enjoy a social life together. Every weekend we would walk the short, quiet country road to visit the local inn for a meal and drink. One evening as we set out it was cold and shrouded in a light fog and so for safety I took a torch. By the time we had decided to return home the fog had descended into a real pea soup, allowing for but a few yards vision ahead. By the roadside we almost tripped over what looked like a dark mound but turned out to be a young man, much the worse for drink, who had decided to curl up and sleep. Without a second thought I asked Jean for a helping hand in getting the fellow to his feet and with his arm around my shoulder, I supported him back to our house. There was not a word of objection from Jean as we cleaned him up and I made him a warm drink of coffee, before laying him on the couch with a pillow and blanket. The following morning after he had a warm breakfast, we sent him on his way. There was a just reward for our action when we returned to the inn the following day in search of my missing wallet. Someone had handed it in having found it by the roadside. The inn owner smiled as he shook my hand, happy to return my wallet and offered us a free meal for helping a friend. Years later Jean would recount what she considered, 'this strange incident' to her friends.

In our different worlds we were unaware of the steep learning curve that we were experiencing. The greatest impact Jean had on me was through her actions, she was not one for telling, just being her kind, loving and gentle self. She had the patience of a saint to put up with me, who was still a child in many ways. There were many splendid things about life I could see clearly see through this child-like perspective and I shared these with her. To my mind it is as though people travelled through the orchard of life and could not even see the fruit, never mind pick it. There are fleeting moments in time that the eye captures, which become everlasting. One such moment occurred when I heard the sound of laughter outside our house one day. As I made my way through the laughing throng of people standing with their backs to me, it was easy to see the cause of their laughter. Our young son Seán was sharing his sheer delight with an audience as he wallowed in mud and water from an outdoor tap. It may well have stirred happy childhood memories for these good German folk. Jean however was not amused as she rushed from the house to see our son's clothes covered in mud, clothes she had earlier changed. My reaction was to dash for a camera to capture the moment.

That year for the Base's Christmas festivities the men put on a musical show with Rusty in a leading role. The singing and dancing was of a high standard with the lads dressed in fishnet stockings, short dresses, wigs and make-up as they high-kicked their way through musical numbers. Sean was old enough to understand a little more about the fun of Christmas and for me to share in his childhood wonderland.

With a baby due in March I took two weeks leave while Jean went into hospital to have our second child. Caring and cooking for our eighteen month old son in Jean's absence was a new and valuable experience that would prove useful in the very long term. It was an experience not without incident. One evening I had bathed and dried Seán ready for bed and while I cleaned up in the bathroom, he made his way downstairs. Holding his pyjamas, I called for him but he was nowhere to be seen, no longer in the house. A roar of laughter from outside sent me running out with his pyjamas still in hand. There he was naked as the day he was born except for my service cap and unlaced service boots on his feet, which he was dragging along the road.

Seán, happily playing in the mud

In late March of 1958 Seán and I visited the British Military Hospital to be greeted by Jean holding a golden-haired little girl, Colleen; our dream was complete with two healthy children. However, the registration of her birth proved to be a problem. When the Registrar discovered that I was from Ireland we were advised to register our child at the Irish Consulate in Bonn, because I as the child's father was not British. The Irish were less than helpful, wanting to know why I was serving in the British Forces. The final option open to us was to register with the German authorities, who welcomed the registration of the birth of our child and provided a birth certificate.

On my return to work at the Base I found major changes in progress. The SIB (Special Investigation Branch) of the military was all over the place like a rash. Talk was rife of a Base member being involved in an incident that took place in the local town and had resulted in an arrest. Many of the men, including myself, were reassigned to new units. For the remainder of my service in Germany I was employed overseeing the running of staff in the Officers' Mess at Geilenkirchen.

While I was based in Germany, I felt it was important that Jean's Mum, as part of the extended family, should be invited to visit and spend time with her grandchildren. The only blood relative I'd kept in loose contact with since our first meeting after my release from the Institution, was my then unmarried thirty-five year older sister, Phyllis. It seemed only right that I acknowledge her as part of our family and so I invited her to join us in Germany on a first family holiday. With a happy healthy family Jean appeared to blossom into an even more beautiful girl and she was thrilled to have her Mum visit to spend time with her grandchildren.

Jean, with our daughter Colleen

Of all the presents I bought Jean in Germany the one that most pleased her was a beautiful electric Singer sewing machine. It was for household and manufacturing use and had combined straight stitching and zigzag, a lamp and other attachments. We were both familiar with the use of sewing machines, Me from my time in Artane and Jean, who had worked in a clothing factory on leaving school at fourteen. I fail to see how Jean's school teachers and many others of the time found their work inspiring or rewarding. Their task was repetitive knowing it was to turn out factory fodder to keep the wheels of commerce rolling. How dull for both teacher and pupil. By contrast my introduction at age ten to making and repairing clothing provided unpaid labour for the Christian Brothers. With the use of the machine Jean displayed wonderful creativity in producing beautiful dresses and overcoats for the children and herself. She would take notes on styles and material colours as she toured dress shops and then produce her own individual styles. Female friends sought her advice and help with alterations to day and evening dresses. Ever popular with her fellow housewives she took to playing tennis and badminton thus enriching her social life. I learned to remain well in the background, so as not to cause embarrassment, or as she would say 'don't show me up'. I was ever fearful of letting slip by word or deed my ignorance in social matters. How could I ever join in a conversation about school, college days, or of my non-existent family background? In spite of these shortcomings I was determined to achieve my perceived ideal of family life by providing the very best loving environment for our family.

Jean, her mother Lilly and Colleen

A deep-seated lack of self worth instilled in me when I was a child, while compensated by the unconditional love from my wife, proved a powerful motivator to enable me to attain my goals. Taking part in sports was a way of both relieving frustration and stress at the lack of progress at a trade to which I was ill suited. In spite of many successes at a number of sports, culminating in winning two national championships and representing my country, the feeling of self worth still eluded me. Without Jean's support I do not believe I could have achieved national success at my chosen sport.

On our return to the UK I decided on a change of career by moving into the Logistics field. My new trade gave me a greater degree of job satisfaction as it suited my mental approach to resolving problems by using cold logic. The change of trade required that I extend my period of service, which I saw as a way of offering a sense of security for me and my family. By signing for an extended period of service I received a financial bonus, which I gave to Jean to spend on herself. This was my way of thanking her for having to put up with my addiction to saving. When she questioned why I was so bent on saving, I explained: "When I see the old folk drawing their meagre pension at the post office, counting the pennies as they struggle to survive, I promise myself that we will not end up so. I will ensure that our old age will be a time to be spent in comfort and security."

In September 1962 the final addition to our family, Karen, was born near our new home in Staffordshire. By the time of her arrival I had assimilated a fair degree of information to help me become a better father. The unforgivable error of beating in order to correct our son I was not about to repeat, I had come to understand that it made me a bully. Such wrongs can never be undone and regrets are long lasting.

On one occasion when Colleen was about five, I was putting her sandals on and she was being uncooperative for which I administered a gentle tap on the leg. She pulled what Jean referred to as 'pet lip' (the lower lip trembles) and tears welled up in her eyes, the sight of which pulled on my heartstrings. Putting my arms around her I told her how sorry I was and promised it would never happen again. Never again did I raise a hand or my voice in anger. In years to come that kept promise would prove to be of great consolation.

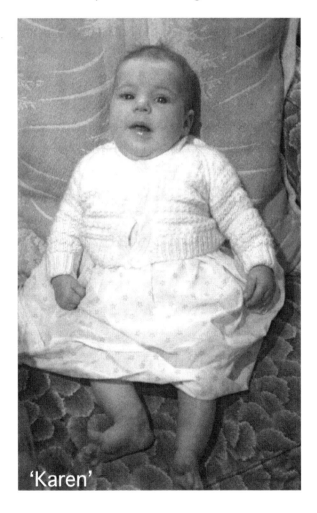

'Karen'

Over the years I continued to discover more of the inner beauty of the girl I married. At our Staffordshire Base we lived next door to a middle-aged couple, a Corporal Gilligan, his wife and their teenage daughter, Maureen. One evening I had just returned home from a cross-country run when a car pulled up and I was asked to help lift Maureen out of the car. The fifteen year old had fainted during school lessons. During the following weeks I noted the absence of the young girl and Jean informed me that she had gone to live with her grandparents. That appeared to explain Jean's constant visits next door. I assumed that she was befriending the couple that were probably missing their daughter. That was until one night some months later, at about eleven o'clock when as Jean was about to pop next door, I remarked: "Come on love, how long are you going to be? I have to be up for work in the morning." To my utter surprise and wonder she reluctantly told me: "I'm taking Maureen to the hospital. Oh! I suppose you'll find out anyway, she's having a baby." Jean continued to mother the young girl and her baby long after they left the hospital. The father was a boy from the same school; they went on to marry and the couple emigrated to Australia and for a time kept in touch with Jean.

Being transferred around the country was an unsettling experience for Jean and our children with the constant changing of schools and friends, but like most things in life nothing comes without its pluses and minuses. I am not sure I would have learned as much had I attended school like our children. I continued my education with daily observations of society at work and play. No more accepting without question what I was being told, read or shown, I retained the inbuilt curiosity of a child.

There was by now no escaping the painful family separations during my service career. Karen was only about eighteen months old when orders to serve in Bahrain arrived. For this posting I was required to be in possession of a British passport and just in time the Home Office produced the British Nationality Act, 1948 section 2(a) to prove that I was a British subject and therefore entitled to one. In spite of these facts, in later life our daughter would be refused the right to a British passport.

On a cold winter's morning in 1963 my small sad family stood in silence at an almost empty railway station, each holding their belongings, and Jean holding the buggy containing Karen, as we waited for the train to take them from me to Jean's family. As I stood holding Jean tight, my heart filled with dread as the train hissed and screeched to a halt. The moment had come to make our tearful goodbyes, knowing it would be a whole long year before we would be together again. Somehow I managed a wave and with a false smile, wished them well as I watched the train pull slowly out of the station. Tears glazed my eyes as I turned to make my way back to my unit with a heavy heart. Knowing they would be settled in the heart of a loving family surrounded by grandparents, uncles, aunts, and lots of cousins to play with went some way to alleviate the pain of parting.

The assignment at my new Base in Bahrain allowed free reign to use my initiative and in addition I was supported in my sporting activities including having the opportunity to fly to Aden to represent the unit at cross-country. I was responsible for a secure, high fenced area, set in a patch of desert that contained two large tents, which were used to offload large consignments of household goods. With a staff consisting of two servicemen and a gang of Yemeni labourers, the crates were unloaded, household goods checked and individual inventories made prior to dispatch to newly open married quarters. With a little imagination I was able to have the empty containers converted into storage racks with shelves on which to store the goods on display. Each shelf had a stapled label containing the description and inventory numbers of the items. To protect the goods against the dust storms a plastic sheet was attached to each rack and weighted down with a wooden batten. This system of temporary storage proved inexpensive, efficient and speedy in supplying demands.

Although there was little entertainment other than the nightly outdoor movies and one visit from a concert group my time flew by. The only act of note in the concert that I can recall was a performance by a large woman opera singer, hardly suitable entertainment for the men. Unappreciative of her performance repeated mock cries of 'more, more' rang out and although everyone was howling with laughter, the poor lady responded by giving them more with repeated encores!

The Middle East tour proved fruitful in so far as my C.O's assessment of my time there resulted in my promotion to fully-fledged Sergeant. It also spelled the end of long service-related family separations.

Enjoying the strange, sights and sounds of a street in Bahrain

On completion of my one year unaccompanied tour in Bahrain I was posted back to my Base in Staffordshire. It appeared that my arrival had been eagerly anticipated. A plan was in the making at an attempt to set a new record for a relay run along the length of Britain. An eight-man team would run non-stop from John O'Groats to

Lands End and I had already been penned in as an essential part of the team. Suffice it to say the eight of us completed the run, non-stop in teams of four, setting the record at that time.

Back together again as a family, Seán and the girls settled in at their new schools. While in Bahrain, I had managed to save money by drawing only enough from my salary in local currency to meet my daily needs. These savings made it possible for Jean, who had learned to drive during our separation, to buy her first good second-hand car. She now had more freedom to visit her parents and pursue her own interests. I devoted extra effort and time to our youngest girl Karen with whom I had a very special bond. She like me was left-handed, but unlike me it would not prove to be a handicap for her. As with proper encouragement she was allowed to flourish. She had learned to read and write before her fourth birthday. I had helped her to recognise letters and the sounds when spoken, just as most parents show their child objects and animals as they relate to names and sounds. Once she mastered letter recognition we enjoyed playing letter games at her pace, first by exploring which two letters made up a word. In time she learned to add a third letter, i.e. 'at' becomes cat, fat, 'no' not. The downside was that she found school boring because it was 'do as I do' 'do as you are told' with no allowance for exploration. Often she would be late home from school but I knew where to find her, at the local library. When I popped into her bedroom late at night I would often find her reading a book under the bedclothes with a torch.

In the 1950s and 1960s wives typically remained at home to raise the family and to do the cooking and cleaning, hence the term housewives. Knowing Jean was happiest working in a factory environment I was pleased for her to have a life outside the house. Once all the children were at school she worked and attained a degree of independence by having her own money. My income was paid into our joint account while I encouraged her to have her own separate bank and account. Throughout our marriage I never inquired or wished to know about her income, as I considered that was her personal business and her rights were to be respected. Some of our savings I learned to invest in the stock and money markets. Whilst serving in Belgium, Germany and Bahrain I had learnt about exchange fluctuations in the money market and took advantage of them. To make additional savings in our monthly budget I applied cost effective methods of shopping with bulk-buying of non-perishable goods. The supermarket era had yet to arrive and household freezers were almost nonexistent. Investing in a large chest freezer proved to be the best economic choice: the normal household freezer had a purchase tax levy while the wholesale chest freezer was tax-free. By buying food and cleaning materials in bulk, considerable savings could be made. All these changes in the methods of running a home were new to Jean; she was set in her ways. At the time, when it came to purchasing more expensive items for the home or general use it was common practice to purchase on what was referred to as the 'never-never', buy now and pay later. When Jean raised concerns about my method of budgeting I had hoped to set her mind at rest with the promise of a better future. My dream goal was to settle down in a large home in the countryside with plenty of land for our family and friends to enjoy.

From my perspective there was too much waste in society; I failed to see the logic in each of the hundred or more married quarters being supplied and heated individually by coal fires. Surely it would have made more sense to have had one central boiler house to supply heating to all the houses? The savings in manpower, transportation and material would have been considerable. It was many years before I was afforded a position of employment to enact the type of improvements that I then saw would bring all round benefits.

Then in June of 1967, we received news of our posting to Singapore: it unfortunately arrived at the same time as a surprise invitation to my sister Phyllis's wedding in Dublin. I was totally unaware that she was going with anyone. As the preparations for our departure were well advanced it was impossible for us to attend the wedding but we did manage to arrange to cross paths in London. Phyllis and her new husband John were starting on their honeymoon with an overnight stop at a hotel. We paid them a short visit prior to checking in at the airport. In the following years we shared visits, thus allowing Jean and our children to see something of the country of my birth.

Our two and a half year tour in Singapore came at that special time and age in children's and parents' lives when the best family memories are experienced. We were provided with a large house, an Amah (a maid) to carry out all household chores and a gardener, just leaving us to take care of the cooking. School and work started in the cool of the early mornings, leaving the late afternoons for swimming, Jean's tennis and my training routine. In the evenings we would mix with the local people at the locals Amah's markets. It was summer clothing weather all year round and even when it rained in the monsoon season the children loved to play out in its refreshing coolness.

On weekends we would explore the island and its parks with the monkeys who would sit next to the children waiting for the chance to snatch food. As we toured the lake, temples and beach I was acutely aware of how special this time was and could not refrain from telling Jean: "We will never experience these moments again. Try to savour the moment before it slips through your fingers like sand."

I was actively involved in sport within the local community, which helped us as a family to make friends and we were often invited to peoples' homes. The sporting authorities accorded me the honour of being official judge at race walking events in which I was not partaking. The rules were simple enough to follow, a heel toe action, with one foot on the ground at all times. The rules for disqualification were for, running or 'lifting' i.e. failing to keep one foot in contact with the ground. At the end of one race my report card added a new and unusual infraction to the rules: 'disqualified for boarding a bus!' How many others may have been successful in shortening their race in this way, I can't say. It was my good fortune to have captured the two fellows' numbers just as they were about to board.

Colleen, Karen and Seán examining sugar cane

We travelled around the country using the popular 'pick-up' taxi, which was exactly as the name implied; the driver picked up as many passengers as his cab would hold. Chinese women never ceased to be fascinated by the colour of our girls' hair, Colleen's golden and curly and Karen's a straw blond. I would pretend not to notice when they could not resist touching the gold curls or bright blond hair. The girls understood the curiosity and just smiled.

One evening as Seán and I were on our way home in a pick-up, we came upon the non too unfamiliar sight of a crowd gathered by the roadside. Our cab joined the curious onlookers that had gathered around the accident scene just to gaze with interest until someone in authority arrived. At the sight of a young girl lying injured and her friend crying, I jumped from the taxi and instructed the crowd to move while Seán gave me a hand to lift the child into the taxi. Acting on pure instinct I ordered everyone out of the way and the driver to proceed to the Base. On arrival at the gates I flashed my ID and insisted on the taxi being allowed in. At the medical centre I shouted for a trolley for the injured child. A member of staff approached, looked at the injured girl and said: "She can't come in here, she's a choge" (a derogatory term for a Chinese person). Hearing that remark stung me into a ranting rage where I threw a few choice words at the man. The disturbance hastened a doctor on to the scene who ordered the child and her friend to be moved inside for treatment. This was not something I wished our son to have witnessed, such shabby treatment meted out to two small children and to see me in a rage. While we waited a local policeman arrived accompanied by a couple. The man was comforting the crying woman and

I guessed they were the child's parents. With the news that the young girl would be okay the woman started bowing, holding her hands as if in prayer while the policeman translated her words of thanks. It made me feel so small and humble and I requested, through the policeman, to hear of her progress in a few days time. Later word did get to me that she had made good progress.

While we lived in Singapore, rather than draw my salary in cash I opened a savings account in the local currency, at a local bank, retaining sufficient cash to meet our daily needs. It proved to be a very wise move in view of the devaluation of the pound sterling towards the end of our tour in 1967-8. Both the interest on the savings, plus the resultant additional sterling currency I received in exchange for the Singapore dollars, were considerable.

It would appear that the original purpose of my assignment to Singapore was to be employed in the explosive department, however someone had forgotten to inform either my unit or myself. Prior to my posting I had attended a specialised course on explosives and gained a qualification in that field. It was not a course I was over enthusiastic about undertaking, bearing in mind it was during a period of great unrest in Northern Ireland. To train me in the explosive field didn't appear to be a well thought out move considering my Irish background. When I expressed my concern to higher authorities in the hope of being excused the course, I was informed: "That's okay we already have a number of qualified explosive Sergeants and they are all Irish, you people appear to have an aptitude for the job!" This was a typical example of the British Monty Python sense of humour that was endemic in many facets of the society that I had come to accept. Although I expressed a willingness to remain in Singapore to perform the task I had been trained for, the error had been discovered too close to the time we were due to return to the UK.

For the first few weeks at my new Base I lived in the Sergeants' Mess while I arranged living quarters for our family. By then I was in regular contact with Phyllis and had given her the Mess phone number and convenient times to call, in case she wished to get in touch with me. When she did call, it was to inform me that her father had died and to ask me if I was going over to Ireland for the funeral. "I'm sorry," I told her "but it would not be right of me to attend, I never knew the man and had not seen him in over twenty odd years." I never knew if she understood my decision not to attend. She had been the only blood relative I had kept in touch with since leaving Ireland in the late 1940s. In view of what little I knew then, my decision should not have come as a surprise. Her sister and I had been 'put away' in 1934, while she was raised by her grandmother and her father's sisters. The first time I found out that I had any relatives was in my sixteenth year. I learned that as her father lay dying he asked to see her 'Mother', his wife. Presumably he wished to express his regrets to her at the break-up of the family sometime in the early 1930s, or to seek forgiveness. Phyllis found herself in a very embarrassing predicament when she introduced her visiting mother to the nurse tending her father. Apparently during an earlier visit another woman with family had already introduced herself to the nurse as Mrs Rice. This was Catholic Ireland where there was no such thing as divorce, but it appears this couple lived happily together as husband and wife, and raised a family of five in state provided accommodation. At no stage did I feel any animosity towards either of my birth parents. How could I? I had never known either of them nor was I aware of the circumstances that led to my abandonment in Industrial Schools at the age of two.

Once we had settled down in Buckinghamshire and our children were back in school, Jean soon found a tailoring job that included collecting and delivering the finished work. In addition to my normal duties I was tasked with preparing men to sit a civil examination in Logistics from the Institute of Purchase and Supplies. To equip me for the task I attended a short local Instructional Technique Course. As this venture was a civilian course it was conducted outside of service hours. Accordingly I was separately reimbursed for my efforts. It was a source of great satisfaction for both students and teacher when all students obtained their qualification certificate from the Institute. The valued certificate could prove to be the key to opening doors to future employment in the Logistics Industries.

Michael Dunne, a fellow Irishman, was the tailoring contractor on the base. When he asked if I knew of any of the service housewives with a tailoring background, I immediately suggested Jean. I knew there was no-one better qualified. In putting my wife forward as a candidate whilst I worked in the general department responsible for contracts, was a cause of concern for him. I had to allay his fears about the possibility of having to let her go, if she proved unsatisfactory after her month's trial period. I suggested he offer her a two-week trial, knowing only too well he would be hard pressed to find anyone better. If during that time he was not one hundred percent satisfied with her work then he should let her go and for my part there would be no recriminations. My problem was then to convince Jean to terminate her current employment for one better suited for her and our family; one that I also suspected offered better pay. For most people the chance of a better offer of employment would not present a problem. However, Jean felt that to accept such an offer would indicate a lack of loyalty to her employer. At first it seemed that no amount of persuasion on my part could change her mind. This was an offer I was not prepared to let pass as it also meant she would only have a short walk to work and would be within walking distance of my workplace. She eventually gave in to my constant late night relentless badgering before I would let her sleep. She had given me her word and I knew that it was golden. It came as no surprise when Michael told me at the end of her first week's employment that she was better than he could ever have imagined. What I had failed to tell him was that she had worked in a clothing factory from the age of fourteen and was still making our own children's clothes, including overcoats. Carrying out alterations and making special fitting uniforms was child's play to her. Within a short period of time he entrusted her with the running of the business and maintaining the associated paperwork.

Over the next two years we spent family vacations with both Jean's folk in County Durham and with Phyllis and her husband in Ireland. Outside of work, while the wives of the very senior officers warmly welcomed Jean at the tennis court, my arrival at the court to take Jean home was a signal for her friends to vanish. Jean failed to notice class barriers, she spoke little but her actions roared with selflessness. She was so vulnerable. On one occasion her boss was very upset with me: "Why did you allow your wife to come to work today? She is ill; she collapsed and I had to take her home in my car." I tried to explain: "I was aware she was ill, but she keeps such things to herself and will keep going until she drops, that is the way she is." By this time I had still to develop some understanding of emotional stress. Jean had received a telegram from home informing her that her Grandmother had passed away. When she told me that she planned to attend the funeral I failed to understand why she would want to travel all that way: "She's dead, there's nothing you can do. I told you before when she was alive; you should have given of your time and presents. Your place is here with our children while they are still young." Her response then had little impact on me but now time, too late, repeats her words in my ear bringing tears to my eyes: "You are one cold hearted bastard!"

As is the way of service life I was suddenly informed that my explosive qualifications were required at a base in Scotland. This was in spite of the fact I had not been employed in that capacity since my training some four to five years earlier. The change to a new location was unwelcome. It was disruptive to the children's schooling, my sporting activities and Jean's life in general, but orders were orders.

When I reported for duty in Scotland, I soon found myself at odds with my new Officer Commanding (OC). The OC waved my objections aside as he informed me that I was to be employed on duties other than my transfer was intended for. His explanation for this change in my intended employment angered me. The Base was near the bottom of the logistics league table in meeting its obligations and I was expected to produce an improvement in its ranking. There were, however, two redeeming factors to this posting: Jean was quickly employed in the tailors shop on the Base while, as before, I was instructed to conduct evening training courses for which I was paid.

To my relief, our stay in Scotland was to be cut short due to an intervention from Training Headquarters. I had returned from some annual leave to be told by one well-meaning chap that a request offering me a post as an instructor at the Logistics Training School had arrived. However my OC had decided to bin the offer, telling me: "You wouldn't be of any use employed there, it's here at the sharp end you are required." Nonetheless, I insisted on being given the opportunity to apply. Although I had no wish to work in the formal setting of a classroom I saw this as my opportunity to move away from a place where we had failed to settle as a family. The department arranged a nice farewell for my wife and I, presenting her with a bouquet of flowers and me with a plaque of the Base. My OC's farewell words were to the effect that he was sorry to lose me so soon after the department had moved into the top three of the league table. In my goodbye message I found it difficult to refrain from laughing as I mouthed the words that I was sorry to be leaving.

Though I was unaware of it at the time, this move to Herefordshire would signal the end of our nomadic lifestyle. There are times when a sight, sound or smell will trigger the release of dark hidden memories of childhood. On one such occasion as we familiarised ourselves with our new home, the sight of a tree heavily laden with yellow blossoms dredged a dark memory back into sharp focus. The death of a child at St. Patrick's Industrial School in Kilkenny, who we had been told had eaten the pods from the tree. As I stood transfixed at the sight, Jean questioned my silence. When I recounted the episode from my past, she told me: "That's a Laburnum and their pods are poisonous." After all this time I was finally able to put a name to the tree.

In early 1973, I was enrolled in a class to learn instructional techniques in order to qualify to be employed as an Instructor. One thing I learned during my stay at the training centre was a degree of self-control. The course, like most courses, made little allowance for the individual approach to teaching. I found it to be a case of, 'do as I do', 'say as I say', little thought was given to the why or how? After a long day in the classroom I usually took a late evening walk into the local town and back. One evening the streets were quite empty except for two young men on the sidewalk walking towards me. As they approached I could sense trouble, they were in an aggressive mood. My first thought was to step off the sidewalk, but just as quickly I knew I could not back down. As we drew closer together I formulated a plan of action. I stopped in front of them and said: "You're not going to let me pass, are you?" They blocked my path and looked menacing: "So, what are you going to do about it?" Stepping back, I asked: "Is it a fight you are after?" This pleased them and in unison they replied: "Yeah, too right." Standing my ground I went on to explain: "I'm happy to take on each of you, one at a time." They looked puzzled as I continued: "The first one to catch me I fight, then the slower one." With that I turned and sprinted off down the road, I stopped and turned as the first one stumbled towards me out of breath, I was then ready to fight. The whole incident came to a sudden halt as a police patrol car appeared from around a corner. One of the officers approached and asked the two men what was happening. Pointing to me one of them reported that I had picked a fight with them. It appeared that the officers were acquainted with the men and when asked for my side of the story I responded: "Is it likely officer that I would pick a fight with two young men much bigger than me?" When asked if I wished to press charges against the men, I replied: "No officer, your timely intervention ended a worthwhile lesson for them this night."

Every weekend during the training course I returned to my family who were living in temporary service accommodation. I had started arrangements to buy our first home, as in fairness to my family I had decided it was time to put down permanent roots. We chose a house that was new, still under construction, and within walking distance of my work place. I chose to buy the property outright in order to maintain control of our expenditure. The fear of any external control in our affairs was strong. My first experience of external influence in our financial affairs was to insure our first born up to the age of sixteen. The final sum paid on maturity was far less than I would have expected had I managed the contributions myself over the sixteen years. From then on I never again took on an insurance policy other than mandatory ones such as for the car. The experience Jean gained whilst working at our two previous Bases proved advantageous in gaining employment once again on this new Base.

Although I successfully completed the instructional course I felt apprehensive about my ability to stand in front of a class of students and attempt to use the techniques I had been taught. In view of some of the students' high academic qualifications I felt a little intimidated and feared I would fail. My first experience of formally instructing a full class was as a stand-in during the absence of the regular instructor. Somehow I managed to stumble through the lesson using the methods I had been trained in. There were times when I wished the floor would open up and swallow me.

When I was assigned my first full class of students to guide them all the way to their final exam, I was absent for their first week. It coincided with an international event I was competing at in Sweden and the Services were always very supportive of sporting activities. On my return to work the first weekly progress examination was due. Once I introduced myself to my students I quickly went through revising the previous week's lessons that had been covered by a stand-in. All my fears vanished as I unknowingly eased into my own natural style of conducting procedures. It was not possible to review the full week's lessons in the detail I would have wanted. It was noticeable that as I continued reviewing the week's lessons some students kept nervously glancing at their watches. They need not have bothered because to their surprise I started to pass around the practical and theory examination papers with the instructions, "take these back to your quarters and I want to see them handed in tomorrow morning with all the tasks completed." As it was Thursday the weekly payday; they would now have little time for beer drinking. The following morning the exam papers showed a very high standard with the exception of two students. My unorthodox method of conducting the exam did not fail to go unnoticed. I was hauled in front of the supervisor and asked to explain my conduct. He had received a complaint that most of the students had spent the evening cheating on their exams. I begged to differ and explained that I viewed the weekly progress test as just that, not a final exam and treated it accordingly. I was of the view that the students had not spent the evening cheating, rather they had arrived at answers through discussion and debate instead of spending their time drinking beer. I asked whether it was not right that once they were employed in the future, they would be wise to question one another when they were unsure about a procedure. My explanation was not well received.

The students soon warmed to my methods of analysing every aspect of a subject under discussion. To introduce my method of teaching I asked that they forget about the classroom procedures they had been told as children. No-one should raise their hand in response to my questions. I would call upon a student whom I wished to answer. Together we would examine each answer given in order to arrive at a logical conclusion. Questions I welcomed and made the point that I did not wish to see a display of ignorance by laughing at a fellow student's question. A word I did not wish to hear repeated was 'remember.' I believed that to question the 'whys' and 'hows' of a subject helped towards discovering and understanding, and negated the need to remember. If learning was not interesting then there was little point to it. I found myself playing the part of a performer rather than an instructor. There was humour to be found in each subject we covered. On one occasion I noticed a girl at the back of the class had fallen asleep, she may have been tired after a long weekend. Putting my finger to my lips, I motioned to the rest of the class to be quiet and waved from them quietly from the room, leaving her to sleep while we visited the canteen.

As we approached the final exam some of my students expressed unease about their chances of success. One thought it had been great fun doing the course but was now fearful of the seriousness of the finals. I advised: "Fear is the unknown; when you understand the subject matter the unknown becomes the known"

The week prior to the final exam I set each pupil the task of preparing an individual set of questions on each topic we had covered during the course. The task was to be undertaken in the evenings. The following morning we would analyze the questions to understand the purpose of the question and to get an insight as to how exam papers were formulated.

The final examination classroom was filled with a palpable silence as the invigilator walked around the room placing exam papers face down on each desk. He outlined the rules of how the exam would be conducted then started his watch at nine o'clock sharp: "Turn your papers; you have two hours starting from now." Standing in the empty corridor outside I could hear the sound of rustling paper followed by a sense of a more relaxed atmosphere. I was confident that they would all achieve good results but hoped that many would receive a distinguished pass.

As the students left the exam room I questioned each of them about the test and they all expressed confidence in passing. One mentioned that he could not contain a fit of the giggles for which he was admonished. He had recalled a humorous anecdote I had used in class to get a point across.

The final course results came as a shock to the supervisor and other instructors. A record had been set for the number of a distinguished passes recorded for one course. All of my students with the exception of two had reached that level. It was common practice for the students with a distinguished pass to be accompanied by their instructor to the Commanding Officer's office, where the students would be congratulated and presented with a badge of promotion. Most of the students gained in excess of 80% in their results. Until that day instructors produced on average one or two distinguished passes per class. It was suggested to me that I was teaching student just to pass exams. However, with the passage of time I was to discover that I had won over both students and the other instructors. My first inkling of this was when John Brown, a fellow instructor, pleaded with me to take his class for an afternoon lesson. When I asked why, he told me: "I promised my class that if they performed well on the weekly tests that I would ask you to take a lesson." Looking somewhat embarrassed he questioned: "Do you know what you're called?" "No" I replied. "They call you the song and dance man, because of the way you teach. Students want to be in your class."

As recently as last year I bumped into John and his wife while out shopping and was surprised when his wife asked me to repeat one special joke I used all those years ago in class to get a point across. Another instructor I came across in the local high street told me that during the Summer he used to open the windows of his classroom, which was next to mine in order to let his class listen to our lessons.

I am often guilty of engaging my mouth before my brain when it comes to matters I feel passionate about, hence Jean's expression 'don't show me up' (embarrass). Such an incident occurred one afternoon while I was out training around the Base grounds, the CO's car pulled up along beside me as I was running:

"Sergeant, you must be very proud of your pupils' results today."

"Not really sir" I responded. "Why ever not?" he asked.

"I failed in getting a 100% distinguished passes." This reply brought the conversation to an abrupt end as his wife looked on speechless when he replied "Quite so" as he pulled away.

For once in my life I had found real satisfaction in my work. In addition to our new home Jean had her first new car, a Vauxhall Cleveite. Settled at last she had no intention of moving again. Our two girls attended their new schools and made friends while our boy, Seán, started at the local Art College. With the success I was having at work I enquired about my promotion prospects. I outlined the exam results, my success at sport and that I had purchased our own house, but these were not considered sufficient to merit reward. The response of my immediate superior officer was: "Yes, you are very good at your job and sport, but you are not a team man. You do not attend functions at the Sergeant's Mess." I saw little point in replying. He failed to understand what it took to achieve National honours at sport and the cost of running one's own home. I could ill afford the time or expense of sitting around drinking beer in the Mess. The time had come for me to consider my future options for I knew my service life was coming to a close.

A decision was forced on me by an incident that occurred one afternoon. It was a warm summer's day when I returned to the base from a twenty-mile workout. At the main gate I was challenged by a young trainee to produce my identity card. As I was stood perspiring in singlet and shorts, I snapped: "For goodness sake man is it likely I would be carrying an identity card dressed like this? You know me?" "Yes Sergeant" he replied and irritated I walked past him "Well don't be so bloody stupid then."

The following morning I was summoned to the Guardroom to find myself charged with disorderly conduct, and failing to produce identity. In my defence I pointed out that at other entrances there were no guards present that it was just my misfortune to leave and enter by the main entrance. The punishment by the Commanding Officer of a fine and a reprimand convinced me that it was time to end my service career by submitting my resignation. Because I had been enjoying my work and lived a short distance away I had used little of my annual leave. It was now time to plan immediate action regarding my long-term future. With my resignation date confirmed I decided on two courses of action. Number one was to seek redress of a grievance against the punishment that I considered too harsh. My second action was to seek temporary local employment with a view to obtaining an insight to an everyday workman's life. While I waited for a date for the hearing of my redress, I took two weeks leave to work in the Mother's Pride local bakery. Though my competitive sporting career had come to an end I continued to run daily to and from the bakery. Starting at the bakery it appeared that a number of men from the Base filled in on shifts during the regular workers' summer vacation time. The work proved to be a salutary lesson in the monotony of assembly line work. There were men employed there all their working lives who were shortly due to retire and who had known nothing else during their working lives.

One of my daily tasks was the mind-numbing, wrist-aching task of speedily transferring the still warm baked loaves as they spewed from the oven, from the rotary roundabout into wire caged trolleys. Different shaped loaves required a different type of trolley to transport the bread to waiting vans. While working a shift loading the bread trolleys with a Supervisor, there was a sudden change in the variety of loaf being produced. Unfortunately in my hurry I fetched the wrong type of bread trolley to the great annoyance of the Supervisor. He asked me how long I had been working there to which I replied a week. His communication skills were somewhat lacking as he spewed forth a torrent of foul and abusive language at me. Rhetorically I questioned; "Is that the only manner in which you know how to communicate?" This brought a puzzled silence before I mused quietly to myself; "I suppose it's not really your fault for you know no different." Later at a canteen break I overheard the episode being discussed and overheard a remark: "That put him in his place." It had not been my intention to upset the Supervisor.

I arrived for the late shift one evening only to be informed that a full compliment of staff was present and as I had been promised two weeks work I would be employed in a cleaning capacity. Soon I had completed the mopping and brushing when I spied the dull brass work along the ovens. Scarcely had I polished some of the brass back to its original state when the manager took me to one side and told me to stop what I was doing and go and find a quiet place to while away the time. It appeared my brass polishing had caused some apprehension among the staff.

On my return to duties at the Base, I found arrangements for my redress had been arranged. I was to report to Training Command Headquarters in London to have my case heard by the Air Officer Commanding. By then I was of the mindset that I was all but finished with the forces as I had a month's leave due, which would end before my final date of service.

Standing in front of this high-ranking officer with more rings up his sleeve than I care to remember failed to make an impression on me. His opening remarks however stirred anger within me. I had felt that I had been treated too harshly by my Commanding Officer and was expecting what I considered an even handed approach to my case. Instead I was greeted with:

"What do you mean by questioning one of my officer's punishments awards?" He was somewhat taken aback when I responded:

"Oh well if I'm in the wrong here I think it best not to precede further Sir" Outraged at my remarks, he told me:

"Sergeant, I don't like your attitude, how in heaven's name did you ever become a Senior NCO?" My reply was out without a thought:

"Sir with great difficulty, anyway I'm finished within a month during which time I'm entitled to undergo a course of training for civilian life. I shall be forgoing that course to spend the time with my family and to seek employment."

There was a pause while his aide had a calming word in his ear and he continued;

"In view of your record I have decided to cancel the fine imposed on you, that is all." I came smartly to attention saluted and thanked him. Before I left to return to my Base one of his young officers remarked that I had done well in having the fine removed, to which I explained I would sooner have had the severe reprimand stricken from the records.

Just as I had left the Industrial Schools of my childhood years I had finished with the services with no regrets or friendships. The forces had served its purpose; it had provided security and a living for my family and I. In addition, I had learned to avoid trouble and taken great advantage of all the sporting facilities on offer. From here on my life and that of my family's was in my hands.

With that in mind from a number of offers of employment, that came my way, I chose a two year contract to work as a Speciality Training Supervisor with the British Aircraft Corporation (BAC) in the Middle East.

Around this time Jean reminded me of the promise I had made her early in our marriage about providing a home of our own and asked if our present one was it.

"No sweetheart, I'm thinking of something much bigger and better and I hope we can retire early to enjoy many years in the home I have in mind." She made it quite plain that her travelling days were over and she was ready to settle down in her new home.

AN EMOTIONAL DISCOVERY

Ever since leaving my country of origin I have never stopped running. Unwilling or unable to accept the fact that I was totally abandoned as a child, I chose to live in denial of a childhood spent locked away in Industrial Schools. The mental and physical acts of running complimented each other. Only after some sixty years, whilst still active and physically running daily on a daily basis, did the mental running came to a halt when in 1999 the Irish Prime Minister's apologised to victims of Industrial Schools and other institutions. My initial reaction was that now he has spoken people would accept that the acts of cruelty inflicted on vulnerable children by a state run by the Catholic Church did take place.

By late 1974 it became a race against time to reach my goal of providing a sound future for our children and plan for Jean and I to retire early. After I left the Air Force Jean also quit her job, but it was not long before she was happily employed with other girls at a local factory. The children had formed close friendships with children from school and the local area. I had bought Seán a new motorbike for his sixteenth birthday, which allowed him a greater degree of freedom to join other youngsters with the same interests. One family in particular, we formed a close relationship with, was a family that had moved into service accommodation on their return from a tour in Singapore. Unfortunately the children's father had failed to return home with his wife and five children. About the same time as their father had completed his tour of duty, he was due for demobilisation and he chose to start a new life in Singapore with a local girl. The only girl of the family became friends with Karen and she spent a lot of time at their house. The eldest of the boys, a sixteen year old, was a member of the circle of friends that included our children. A number of the boy bikers and some of the girls wore leather jackets but this sixteen year old stood out because of his PVC jacket. He became known as 'Plastic Man.' His mother was being hurried to vacate her service accommodation and in addition was having financial problems. Jean, as always, was on hand to help out. Her children were after all friends of our lot. Our oldest girl, Colleen, had finished school and started work at sixteen, Sean at eighteen and Karen twelve, were still in education. I decided for purely financial reasons to accept a two-year employment contract in the Middle East. Before my departure I accompanied Jean home to visit her Mother who was ill in hospital suffering with cancer. It was the last time I would see this very special woman alive. As we looked into each another's eyes she could read the sadness I was feeling, she smiled as she thanked me for looking after her daughter. From the first day I met this lady I always felt a welcoming warmth about her. She had shown a faith in me that only her daughter shared.

My post with the British Aircraft Corporation was as a Speciality Training Supervisor of Logistics for Saudi Air Force personnel. The role entailed the supervision of OJT (on the job training) that was conducted by ex-British service personnel. The daily duties were carried out by the trainers who had been of equal or lower rank to the men they were training. The organisation bore no resemblance to any western concept of a military structure. To best describe its structure would be to take the way most people would perceive the way a military Base is run and turn that perception on its head. In this Air Force there were no 'other ranks', all new entrants started out as Warrant Officer grade three and over time reached the rank of Chief Warrant Officer. All the Air Force personnel went home around midday at the close of work whilst all the civilian trainers and support personnel were housed on Base in the barrack blocks. A number of trainees had other outside business interests in addition to their service careers. On one occasion during a morning inspection round, I witnessed the officer in charge of the Logistics department become involved in a dispute with one of the senior trainees. The man's desk was covered in bank notes that he was counting and placing in a briefcase. From what little Arabic I had learned, I understood that the officer was telling the trainee that he was not there to conduct his private business. The end result was that the upset trainee scooped the remaining money into his briefcase and left for home. It was quite common for trainees to either arrive late or fail to turn up for 'duty.' Regular absenteeism resulted in the offender being sentenced and confined to barracks to serve his detention in the guardhouse on Base. The Base and guardhouse security was maintained by army personnel and it was a strange sight to Western eyes to observe a guilty Warrant Officer trainee being 'escorted' by an army private to serve his 'punishment' as they both strolled hand-in-hand on their way to the guardhouse. I was further surprised to learn that during their term of confinement the trainees were waited upon hand and foot by their army guards. Some I understood considered it as a break from their family life.

There were about a dozen Specialty Training Supervisors, one for each wide-ranging Air Force speciality. From our shared offices we often observed the trainees arrive by car each morning. The service work area was some distance from the Base guardroom by the main gate. Cars entered the work area by road. As they approached the army-manned barrier, a guard wearing an ill fitting uniform and wearing boots without laces would blow a whistle and signal by holding up the red side of what looked like a large tennis bat. He would then proceed to raise the barrier followed by displaying the green side of the bat to enter. Few drivers waited to watch such a futile exercise and just drove over the compacted sand either side of the barrier. It was obvious that some of these poor army fellows had yet to become accustomed to wearing boots or could it be that they were so ill-fitting that some had either cut out the back or aired their feet by standing on the heel piece?

To complete the training contingent, a number of Pakistan Air Force personnel were employed to wander around checking the training. They were all of Sergeant rank or above and reported to their own officer who in turn reported to the Saudi officer in charge, a Captain Koradji. For long periods I found my work deeply frustrating. A lot of the time I wandered around speaking to the trainees, trainers and Pakistani personnel. It was not long before I was to discover the limited general knowledge that one of the Pakistani men possessed. During a general conversation he expressed doubts about the Americans having landed a man on the moon. When he started talking about snow I have to admit I was intrigued by his perceptions and could not control the urge to have a bit of fun:

"What does it feel like in all that white snow?" he asked me,

"it looks lovely, is it very cold?"

"It's not all white snow; sometimes it's black and slushy."

"Do you mean there are different colours of snow?"

"Why yes, there's red snow in Russia, Green in Ireland."

I could see he was taking it in and could not resist becoming more outrageous. Pointing to my liquid crystal watch, I asked: "Do you know how the Japanese make these small watches with batteries?" Wide-eyed he indicated he did not.

"They breed these special very tiny men and women, like little ants that can fit inside the watch and put all the parts together."

Stifled giggles could be heard from some of the nearby trainers and his immediate superior motioned him away. I was later hauled in front of Captain Koradji to answer a complaint from the officer in charge of the Pakistani men. I was extremely fortunate to have earlier made a favourable impression on the Captain who dismissed the complaint as a bit of fun.

During one of my rounds of the sections I came across a large number of aircraft spare parts in the trash. When I questioned why so many of one particular item had been disposed of, I was informed that their life-time had expired. A check of the provisioning and stock control records revealed that only a handful of the items had been used during the past year. This indicated over provisioning, unnecessary loss of money to the Saudi Authorities and profit to the contractor. When I brought this to the attention of the Captain he informed me that he was aware of the expired items and questioned why I should speak against my company: "Is that not being disloyal to your firm?"

"Sir, my job is to train your men in stock

control, provisioning and best practices. It is not a question of loyalty but a question of what is right. It is best your men learn early to avoid over ordering otherwise next time it may be more expensive equipment wasted." To my great embarrassment he gathered all the trainers around and pointed to me: "I wish more of you would follow this man's example and do your job and not just come here to collect money."

After that incident the Captain and I worked closer together and I was intrigued by the manner in which he conducted himself at the monthly meetings of the different sections heads within his departments and the manager representing the company BAC. He wore dark glasses at these meetings and watched as he asked confrontational questions. He would then sit back and quietly observe with interest how different points were being debated. When I questioned him about the dark glasses after one meeting, he explained that he liked to observe the intensity and passion in people's eyes as they spoke about their interests. He believed that the glasses prevented others from noting his reactions, I remarked: "You like to play devil's advocate I notice." He asked me to explain what that meant and when I did he was pleased to learn and made a note of the two words.

During my first year abroad I received the sad news that Jean's Mother had passed away. As soon as Jean was informed that death was imminent Seán and Karen accompanied her on the journey to be by her Mum's bedside. By then Seán was driving which eased her load, unfortunately they just failed to say their last goodbye in time. The best I could do was to keep in touch by telephone and letter until such time as I arrived home on vacation. There was no possible way I could begin to imagine the grief and pain she was undergoing at the loss of her Mother. During my vacation I accompanied Jean to her family home to visit her Mum's last resting place. For a week of the vacation I arranged a surprise holiday for Jean and I in the City of Rome. With Seán and Colleen still living at home they were capable of looking after Karen. I had made the effort to learn enough Italian to help us get by. I booked us into the Grand Hotel Beverly Hills, one of the City's finest. We took in all the sights of the city and the Vatican and in the evenings we took a train ride to relax by the seaside.

Towards the end of my contract I had noticed rapid changes taking place in our family. Colleen at eighteen and Seán, nineteen had both found partners and were in serious relationships. During my homecomings I spent a considerable amount of time in Karen's company. She was a bright intelligent child for her age. Social attitudes were changing and I was concerned for her welfare:

"If you ever find yourself in the frightful position of becoming pregnant I want you to promise me that I will be the first person you come to. That is a time a young girl requires all the support and love of the family."

"I know that Dad, you need not worry," she told me.

On the Base all ex-patriots had to be very careful in their daily conduct towards the trainee Warrant Officers. It was their country, their Air Force; they were Officers and expected to be treated as such. Unfortunately one 'Officer' took advantage of the situation and treated me with contempt. In a lightening flash I had punched the lad in the waist. He tried to brazen it off by showing he could not be hurt by the likes of me but he failed to keep up the pretence and sought the assistance of a fellow Officer nearby.

For my actions I was summoned by the Training Manager to appear in front of the Captain. The Manager feared for my future: "You are aware this will mean at least a window seat for you." This expression referred to being shipped home on an aircraft.

Present in the Captain's office in addition to myself, were the Manager and the Officer in charge of the Pakistani personnel. It was the latter who had brought the complaint against me. I was somewhat taken aback by the Captain's approach:

"Now then Paddy what have you been up to?"

"I'm sorry sir I just lost control; I will offer an apology to the young man."

"You'll do no such thing." He told me to my surprise, "I understand he was disrespectful to you. Next time I want you to hit him harder, I will not have my men treat you with disrespect." As the Manager and I left the office, he questioned: "How do you get away with something like that?" The only answer I could come up with was the word: "Respect."

It was not long before we were both back in the Captain's office again. This time the Captain was requesting that I renew my contract. He failed to understand that it was not a decision I could take without consulting my wife. He instructed the Manager: "See that this man and his wife are allocated accommodation of their choice and meet his salary requirements." I made a promise to consider a further year's extension to my contract but first I had to discuss the matter with my wife. On what should have been the final vacation of my contract I talked over the offer with Jean. There was no budging her on her original decision that her days of travelling were over and we mutually agreed to a one-year extension of my contract.

By way of compensation I thought it would be a nice gesture to buy Jean a new car. Not just any car but one we had talked about when we first met. She had told me how on one occasion she and her other young girl friends had their noses pressed against a car showroom before they were chased away. They had been playing make-believe by picking their own favourite car; Jean's was a red Rover. The car we had bought two years earlier failed her within one week when the shift stick came off in her hand as she drove around a roundabout. A replacement car had failed to boost her confidence in the model.

At a prearranged meeting at a car showroom I explained to the salesman that I was purchasing the new Rover as a surprise for my wife. I instructed that when we arrive to look around he should invite her to take a test drive. On arrival at the garage I asked Jean if she would like to 'have a go' in the car: "Oh I couldn't, it's a bit too posh for me." True to form the salesman played his part and coaxed her to take a test drive. When she returned, I asked: "How did you find it"? She was thrilled to have driven the model of her childhood dream. I took the keys from the salesman: "It's yours sweetheart." She could scarcely believe it was hers; it took some time to sink in. It was years later that one of her work colleagues related the story of the day she first took the car to her workplace. The girls were discussing the fancy car parked in the lot. Some thought it belonged to a visiting boss of the company. When Jean was nudged and asked her opinion as to whom the owner might be. She looked very embarrassed and reluctantly admitted that it was hers, given as a gift from her husband.

Prior to my return to work Karen asked if she could have a small dog as a pet to which I agreed. It was a small scruffy creature that resembled a floor mop and required house training. I warned Karen that she had better have it trained by my next visit because it was continually wetting the kitchen floor. On my return little progress had been made in house training the dog and she appeared not unduly upset at having to find it a new home. I later discovered she had given the dog to her girl friend's family. The family had moved from the Base accommodation but the family friendships remained. The eldest boy 'Plastic Man' had not long finished his schooling when he formed a relationship with a thirty-year-old woman who had three children. They later married when he turned seventeen. When I enquired of Karen about the welfare of the dog and if was still wetting around their house, she told me: "No Dad it's doing fine there, they let it sleep in the bed with them. It has stopped wetting the floor, now it wets the bed."

Seán getting into Jeans Red Rover as she looks on

That final year abroad passed swiftly with having so much to look forward to on my home visits. Our daughter, Colleen, was married in March and Jean was kept busy with the wedding arrangements. Seán had moved into accommodation he shared with other students. Over time students came and went, one left without notice leaving his dog behind. The dog, Bob was to fulfil one of Seán's dearest wishes to have a dog of his own, a wish that we could not entertain until then due to our unsettled lifestyle.

In spite of completing an additional year to my original contract I was still being urged to reconsider the offer of a new and better contract to remain with the company. No amount of money or inducement could keep me apart from my family any longer. I had already given one daughter away in marriage and I could see our son would shortly follow. My main consideration was to devote as much time as was possible to Karen. My contract completed, I returned home in time for her fifteenth birthday on 12th September. In addition to the present of a new bike for her birthday Jean and I agreed that Karen and I should take a two-week vacation in Ireland. In order to avoid disruption to her schooling, it would have to be after our twenty-second wedding anniversary. There were also both our birthday celebrations to consider on 7th and 8th October and so it was that the flight tickets were ordered for 20th October during her school break. In the weeks leading up to our vacation we were rarely out of one another's company. As we talked and walked along the country roads I found her to be a bright intelligent girl beyond her fifteen years. For the second time I broached the subject of pregnancy, she laughed it off: "Dad I know you would be there for me but it's never going to happen."

For our birthdays she presented us with a pair of statuettes; one of a smiling lady holding a large silver cup and inscribed on the plinth with the words: 'World's Greatest MUM'. The other statue was of a man with a bow tie, wearing a gold crown and inscribed at the foot with: 'World's Greatest DAD'.

After our evening meal on 19th October, Jean was in the kitchen washing the dishes; Karen was in her bedroom starting to pack for the morrow while I was in the sitting room. I overheard Jean call, "Karen will you give me a hand here with the dishes?" It was met with a lazy reply, "In a minute." "Now please." "In a minute," was her irritated reply. I interrupted by telling Jean that I would get her to come down. Karen agreed to help me do the dishes and we chatted about our forthcoming vacation as we worked. Jean and I decided to take a walk along the country roads at about six o'clock before turning in for the evening. Karen was to visit Seán to take his dog Bob for a walk with her friend next door but one. Prior to leaving with Jean I was excited about our vacation and gave Karen a hug and kiss: "We're going to have a wonderful time in Ireland with no expense spared."

Hardly had we entered the house on our return when the phone rang and a voice at the other end said there had been an accident about half a mile up the road from our house. The rest of the words I failed to catch, we jumped into the car and Jean drove. It was still light between six thirty and seven o'clock. Karen had been hit by a careless RAF driver who had left the scene of the accident where we were confronted with the sight of Karen lying in the road. Instinctively and unspoken I think we both knew we had lost her. I had witnessed the same scene in my childhood of a child who had been knocked down and killed during my years in Artane Industrial School. There was blood trickling from both her mouth and ear. I panicked and ran to the nearby Medical Centre at the RAF Base, where I was informed that an ambulance was on its way. Not a word was spoken as we followed the ambulance to the hospital. We sat silently holding hands in A&E waiting, but we did not have long to wait to hear the fatal words: "Sorry we lost her." From that moment I was no longer strong, I fell apart, crumbled like sand. No comfort to anyone I recall requiring medical treatment. For the first time in my life I cried uncontrollably and suffered pins and needles all over my body. There is little I can recall of the following hours or days. All I wanted to do was to get away by running each day till I dropped. No comfort or good to anyone else or to myself. I turned to Jean seeking some understanding of my unbearable pain: "What is this? I feel as though someone has reached into my chest and ripped my heart out." I asked, "When will it end?" Years later our daughter told me that her Mom knew I would refuse to take any medication so she mixed it into my food. It was no wonder I managed to sleep and walked around in a trance for days.

Oblivious to my surroundings Seán, who had just turned twenty-one, took on the mantle of head of the family. He contacted all of Jean's family members and handled the funeral arrangements. I can recall agreeing to his suggestion that I should purchase a graveyard plot for three. All of Jean's family members and friends arrived to attend the funeral service. The one representative to attend from my side of the family was my sister Phyllis. Years later I was to learn of the shock and hurt I caused to my immediate family by my reaction to the death of our daughter, their younger sister. In their eyes I had been a pillar of strength, someone to comfort them in their time of need. Then at their greatest time of need I proved to have feet of clay, a whimpering fool unable to even care for myself. A chance remark: "You're a lot of use" went unheeded then, but the remark would serve as a reminder of a vulnerability I was unaware of until that day. Jean took some time off work and tried to console me but to little effect as all I wished to do day after day, was to run and run until I dropped and then sob my heart out. Our house became a reminder of a shattered dream from which I wanted to run and run, I did not want to spend time there. I chose to get away to my sister's home in Ireland for a while. Both Phyllis and her husband left me alone to come to terms with my loss by wearing myself out, running along the local beach. Up and down sand dunes I ran until I could no longer stand, then I dropped and cried until there were no more tears. By the time I returned home to Jean I had recovered somewhat and presented her with a large Waterford Crystal lamp as a token of my love for her.

In the year following our loss I sought employment locally. Of two positions I was offered, one as a postman which I turned down. The other was in the insurance industry; I attempted it but could not envisage myself spending a month in that line of work never mind the remainder of my working life. After about ten months out of fulltime employment it was time to start back again. Just short of my forty-eighth birthday, my prospects of employment at home were limited and so I opted once again for employment in the Middle East where my proven work experience was in demand. Aiming high I applied for the post of Inventory Management Supervisor with Lockheed Aircraft Corporation in July 1978. Though I did not possess the normally required Bachelor's Degree in Business Administration or Accounting, as outlined in the description for the post, it did not stop me applying. I felt I possessed the required experience. My application was successful and I was invited to start on 24th August 1978. The decision proved to be a change in my future for the better because the new employment provided the opportunity for me to reach my full potential.

There was still time before my departure to set about looking for that new home in the countryside. With just two of us remaining in a house that was now silent of the sounds of children and in their place only reminders everywhere triggering painful memories of a loss too painful to bear, urging me that it was time to move on.

One of Jean's workmates had talked wistfully of a house in the countryside that she and her husband very much wished to buy. They could ill afford to buy the property because it consisted of more than one house and land. I could not pass up the temptation to view the property. As we drove from the town emerging green fields and woodland greeted us. We turned off the main highway along a narrow snaking road that was overshadowed by trees. To one side a patchwork of green fields sloped down towards a meandering river. To the other side of the road woodland reached as high as the eye could see. No sooner had we arrived at the property then I knew that it was the place I could transform into my long held dream home. Jean viewed the property as it existed, a muddy dirt track leading from the narrow road to the rear of the property. The main living quarters required a lot of renovation as did the cottage, a double tier warehouse and the overgrown land required clearing and landscaping. To my eye I could envisage a new driveway, the land landscaped with many fruit trees and all the buildings transformed into well-maintained units.

There and then I decided to purchase the property in spite of Jean's reservations. When she wished to know why we required such a large property, I told her of my vision of our future grandchildren enjoying the fresh air and open spaces. Though she doubted the prospects of the arrival of future grandchildren, she trusted my judgement.

Once again on 10th August 1978 Jean and I found ourselves sitting in the same hospital we had been in just a short ten months earlier awaiting the sad news of Karen's passing. On this occasion Colleen gave birth to our first grandson, Lea. It was truly a new page that had been opened in our lives.

We were fortunate in agreeing the quick sale of our house but I was unable to conclude the transactions relating to the sale of our house and purchase of the new properties prior to the date of my departure. By designating our son with the Power of Attorney I was able to delegate and instruct him on all the arrangements and to sign the legal documentation on our behalf. I arranged our first small mortgage plus funds for him to manage towards the commencement of building work.

Plans to settle down were still some time off yet; rather it was a time to work towards our dream retirement. Partings were sorrowful but reunions were bliss. Jean still chose to remain at home and by then I had learned that all life was not without a positive and a negative aspect. Through the horrendous emotional experience of the unexpected loss of a child I had suffered for the first time the raw hurt of emotional pain. Slowly

I came to accept that I had become imbued with an essential missing function, the ability to cry bitter tears. Physical hurt I had learned to cope with from an early age.

The regular partings over the next few years gave us an appreciation of the precious quality time we did spent together. My new work I found both challenging and satisfying and my American work colleagues were generous and friendly. I was given a free hand to assess the system and shortcomings in the Jeddah Logistics Department systems, as they existed. As a result of my assessment I concluded the whole system required overhauling. In order to develop and implement an improved material management system I would have to work long and hard in my own time. I needed to keep myself occupied both physically and mentally. In the late evenings and weekends I went on long runs across the desert. The first few months flew by and on my first vacation we attended our son's wedding on Boxing Day of 1978. The couple made good company for Jean at our new home. Jean had settled in well at home, had a good social life at work and became a member of a local badminton club. It was important that I should not disrupt her social life on my visits home. I had seen marriages break-up due to men wanting their wife's full attention whilst they were home on vacation. When they returned to their work and friends, their wives then had to pick up the threads of their social lives after a month's break.

Bedouin encampment

PURSUIT OF A DREAM

My assignment at Jeddah lasted one year but flew by. In that short period of time I introduced and organised a new logistic and procurement function to support the Company's programmes at their Jeddah, Medina, Khamis Mushayt and Taif Lockheed sites. This required the hiring and training of new staff plus the design of documentation to achieve the objective of making the new department functional. My responsibilities for running the department consisted of: shipping support materials, household goods and personal effects to and from the USA and UK. In addition, the role included the procurement from local contractors and from the USA of all items to support both the Program's Mission and the requirements of the Support Services. They also included the warehousing of all supplies and materials, and the stock and property control accounting following the receipt and issue of items.

The work environment was warm and friendly which helped to ease the ache I was still feeling after the loss of our daughter. Many evenings after my work-out, I visited American families to check on the progress of their personnel effects that had been shipped from the States. Shipments were often held by local Customs at the Docks and in spite of my best endeavours in meetings with the shipping contractors I had little success in releasing them in a timely manner. Many families complained about their personal effects arriving almost halfway through their contract whilst a small number were unfortunate in finding their effects about to arrive towards the end of their work contract. In the hope of speeding up the process I hired a local Saudi to liaise with the local Customs Authorities. It would not be wrong to describe this guy as a regular wheeler-dealer. He had a ready smile that displayed a mouth full of gold and with an out-stretched hand emblazoned with heavy gold rings, money whispered when he was around. He was sharp enough to feel slighted on one occasion when after shaking hands with him I counted my fingers in jest.

I was working in the office one weekend, that is to say the Arabic weekend of Thursday and Friday, when it appeared that the US office had sent an official over to Jeddah to look into the mounting complaints about the late arrival of personal effects. After a quick inspection of my department I was invited to join in a meeting with the Manager of Facilities, Engineering and Services. The official asked how I would go about resolving the problem and as I started to put forward my thoughts, the Manager interrupted me. He was asked to be quiet whilst I suggested my solution to the problem. The resolution as I saw it was straight forward, the transportation of personnel effects by sea should be totally dispensed with and the personnel allowances for air shipment should be increased. There would then be a need to furnish family accommodation locally. A signed inventory could be compiled for each house, with one copy retained by the occupant and one maintained in the inventory office. In addition each employee should receive a small allowance to purchase soft furnishings. I later discovered that my general recommendations were introduced and proved to be both cost effective and efficient. The company's contract with the Saudi Government was further secured when it won a lucrative contract and at the time plans were already underway to build a new complex in Jeddah: 'Lockheed City'.

I enjoyed working in Jeddah but it would be true to say that I was separated from my American colleagues by a common language. On arrival at my office after a hard working weekend I was asked by one of the women how I'd spent the weekend. My answer was greeted with puzzled looks and laughter: "I've been humping furniture all weekend." The statement that I wished to order a number of jugs was greeted with smiles: "What size do you want?" My innocent reply brought howls of laughter: "You know normal size milk jugs." It appears they knew what I was referring to as pitchers. I swiftly learnt the importance of knowing the different terminology and spellings in order to clearly communicate via I.D.C.s (Inter Departmental Communications).

With my task at Jeddah completed in just under a year, the department was handed over to a newly arrived American Manager, prior to my transfer to Headquarters at Riyadh. I retain very fond memories of my time at Jeddah. The warm friendship and generosity shown to me by my American hosts will always remain with me. I was very privileged to be invited into people's homes during the Thanksgiving festivities to celebrate with them.

I arrived in Riyadh in July of 1979 and worked through Christmas into the New Year. It was unfortunate that I missed the birth of our first granddaughter, Kerri. She was born in our house on New Year's Eve to our son and his wife. I did however make it home two months later for the birth of our daughter's second boy Jay. Now we had three grandchildren.

By the end of June 1980 I was meant to complete my Salaried Work Review Statement. I was instructed not to complete it by the Director of Logistics, a Mr D. G. Bussey. He decided that only he could best do justice to an assessment of my year's work. The following are some extracts from his review: Developed and implemented an improved material management system, including training of personnel to operate the system in a short period of time. He established an operational warehouse including development of a good working relationship between all employees in the warehouse area, the delivery crew, warehouse men and stock record clerk. Revised the delivery service to out-lying sites to achieve a more efficient and economical service.

Developed and published a revised catalogue for common parts, household goods and stationary items. The system is operating efficiently and has reduced manpower requirements on the part of the requisitions and supply activities. The Material and Procurement department was reorganised. In accordance with a Saudi Labour Law directive female employees were replaced with T. C. N's (Third Country Nationals), and all employees trained and qualified in their assigned tasks. He has proved to be a dynamic and effective leader.

The daily challenges I encountered at work kept my mind occupied and helped me with the grieving process following my loss. The confidence placed in me to carry out the changes I had envisaged, and seeing the successful results of my efforts, provided me with great job satisfaction. My contract with the firm was open ended and as long as I was happy, I was prepared to continue working to reach my goal of retiring to our dream home. In addition to my normal duties at Riyadh I was assigned the responsibility of Acting Manager at both Riyadh and Jeddah for a total period of four months. These assignments took place when the Director or one of the Managers was on a leave of absence.

Over the next two years I was given a free hand to introduce changes in the different sections within the Logistics Department. Over a period of time during my visits to one warehouse, I couldn't fail to notice the countless number of times members of the vehicle maintenance shop approached the cleaner for advice on vehicle parts. It appeared this chap, who was employed sweeping the warehouse, was a highly qualified mechanic back in his home country. When I asked him why he was working as a cleaner, he told me: "There was no work at home in the Philippines to support my family. When I applied for work here there were no vacancies in my trade." I arranged for the man to be transferred to the Vehicle Maintenance Department to the delight of the Manager there. It was not long before the man was promoted to the position of supervisor.

With the introduction of a new Director of Logistics my career came to an abrupt end. I had discovered an American employee had placed a priority order in the States for aircraft equipment without first checking the local in-country company warehouses. He had failed to understand the man-hours and expense involved in shipping a priority item from the USA. The Director informed me that; "You got your nose out of joint with an employee and I'm not prepared to tolerate that, I will have to let you go." I concluded that the new Director had failed to appreciate two statements recorded on my last review; that I was hard taskmaster in training my subordinates and that I was demanding but fair. Trying to put the case for my behaviour proved futile. The employee was better paid than his fellow T.C.N. workers. By demanding better of him and by castigating him I guess I had got 'my nose out of joint'.

In accordance with the terms of my

contract I was to serve three months employment termination notice, during which time I was given a 'lateral move' and downgrade of company vehicle. Many employees in these circumstances decided to return home without completing the notice period. To do so meant forgoing an agreed bonus payment, plus I would have considered it a failure to quit. I knew no better than to apply myself to whatever task I was assigned.

A month later I was summoned to the Director's office. He was curious about the manner with which I approached my work. I was not prepared to tell him that the one reason I was so committed was to keep me occupied so as to avoid dwelling on my loss. Of course I mentioned that I enjoyed the challenge and that it gave me job satisfaction. It came as a surprise to be informed that the Site Manager wished me to be appointed as Acting Manger while he was absent on his upcoming vacation. I pointed out my lack of experience and mentioned that he had a number of Supervisors he could delegate. Nonetheless the Director informed me that it was I he wished to act as his deputy in his absence. The result of my time in the post was to later open up new opportunities for me within the company.

Unknown to me, my Director had received correspondence from the Vice President and Program Director of Ground Engineering and Navigational Aids (GENA), regarding the many support problems that existed at two compounds situated in Khamis Mushyat. In the correspondence he listed seven areas that were causing him grave concern and one urgent problem regarding the lack of support to the Saudi Air Force due to the number of unserviceable vehicles. On 3rd July 1982 the new Director of Facilities, Engineering and Services (FES) invited me to consider travelling to Khamis Mushayt to undertake a special assignment to resolve these problems. Though I had but a little over a month left of my employment I was happy to accept the challenge. With clear flight instructions and a list of tasks to be undertaken I arrived at Khamis on the fifth of the month after travelling from Riyadh to Abha the local airport. The instructions authorised me to hire six labourers for fifteen days at 15 Riyals (equates to £3), per hour for eight hours a day. My instructions also included the organisation of compound security by ensuring the local Arab Gate Guards were conversant with their duties. That was one problem that would have far reaching effects further down the line. The instructions strongly emphasized that I was to co-operate fully with the Site Manager, and to report progress to Riyadh at regular intervals.

The city of Khamis Mushayt is located in the south west of Saudi Arabia. With a mild climate it is the agricultural region of the country. Its name is derived from the weekly market that is held each Thursday and Khamis is the Arabic for Thursday. Mushayt refers to the local tribe. It was one of six Air Bases in the region. The mild climate was a pleasant change from the dry warmth of 40 degrees Celsius plus of Riyadh. It was mountainous, two thousand meters above sea level with heavy rains and thunderstorms in March and August. The average temperatures from May to September were 26 to 30 degrees Celsius and lows during December and January of 18 to 8 degrees.

The sites consisted of a bachelor complex and a separate family site. Both sites were about seventy-five percent occupied. The unoccupied villas were in a poor state of repair and abandoned furniture littered the flat roofs.

I managed to complete my assignment to the full satisfaction of the residents and the Site Manger within a two-week period prior to my return to Riyadh. By letting it be known during my assignment that I would be out of contract the following month, I received a number of offers of employment from different companies. It was rewarding to be aware of a clamour for me to be retained permanently at the sites. Much later I was to learn that a meeting had taken place between the General Manager of Sites and the Khamis GENA Site Manager regarding the possibility of my being offered the duties of Site Superintendent of Khamis Mushayt. The Director of FES was quite satisfied that I had the ability to carry out the tasks related to the post.

When summoned to the Director's office to be offered the position of Superintendent I was somewhat taken aback. Though I was pleased, I asked for time to consider the offer. My first thoughts were of returning home to spend time with my family and to discuss future employment plans with my wife. There were also a number of other offers of employment to consider and only a matter of days in which to decide. In addition to the Director's offer I had reduced my options to three. There was an offer from Saudi-Tel, but they wanted me to start within days. The other offer was of a Logistics Manager's post with the firm involved in the construction of a new airport at Riyadh. The Director of FES generously offered to provide transport and a driver to take me to and from the arranged interview with the construction firm. His action tended to sway me towards accepting his offer providing it was possible to make a few minor detailed alterations to the contract. My interview with the construction firm completed I promised to advise them of my decision within a day. To accept the post would have been a huge challenge and a step into the unknown.

As a result of negotiations between the Director of FES and the Site Manager at Khamis, the Director informed him in writing that he was satisfied with my ability to carry out the tasks and also accepted the conditions of the post as outlined by the manager. He did not agree however with the suggestion that I report to the Area Manager. He also requested the approval of the Vice President/Program Director of GENA to the amendments to the original arrangements. The result of the agreement meant that I had the authority to implement changes on the Sites that I considered were necessary and that I would report directly to the Director of FES at Riyadh Headquarters.

On the 25th July 1982 I returned to Khamis as the newly promoted Site Superintendent with instructions that the outgoing incumbent was to assist me by working with me for the duration of his employment termination period. During the first two weeks I made mental notes of all the changes and improvements that I intended to carry out. By then my original end of contract vacation was due and it had been agreed that I would take it prior to the start of my new contract.

Instead of returning home unemployed I was overjoyed to report to my wife that I had been promoted and given a new two-year employment contract. It also meant that I was well on my way to achieving my goal of early retirement. There was still no convincing Jean to accompany me on my travels and I was not about to try. By the end of 1982 we had another grandchild, a girl bringing the total to four. It would appear that the dream of sharing in the joy of children frequenting our home during our retirement was coming true. During my vacations home I endeavoured to avoid disrupting Jean's activities. She carried on playing her badminton and kept company with her many work friends. Though she had no need to work, she wanted to and it was her choice. There was still the deep pain of partings but our quality time together was sheer bliss.

On my return to the Site, as I first entered the main gates I had formed a clear vision of how I intended the whole area to appear and function after the wholesale changes I planned to introduce. It was evidently possible to grow grass, as in some areas a few small flowers and trees blossomed, some small areas of the sites were overgrown, whilst others lay barren with sand and scrub. The odd handful of villas using water sprinklers with recycled water had well-maintained gardens.

Some villas had problems with dampness on their interior walls. Over the years much time and effort had been spent trying to eliminate the problem using damp resistant materials, such as that used on swimming pool walls. A number of possible reasons for the cause of the damp had been recorded. One was that the location of the villas made them prone to the direction of the wind and rain during the wet season. The source of the problem was staring at us in the face, the sprinklers! The only villas affected were the few that possessed sprinklers. The water was splashing against the walls that were made of pebble-dashed porous breezeblock on the outside and plastered inside. A cost effective way of avoiding the problem was to create a pathway of coloured stone chips around the villa walls. The greater areas of both sites were carpeted with a little scrub and sand, the reason I was told was due to the shortage of water. The water for the sprinklers was recycled water from the site's Sewerage Treatment Plant. The fresh water supply was delivered daily under contract by tankards to underground storage tanks. A check on the monthly water supply bill revealed a large disparity between the volume received and that recycled. An investigation of the waste flow through drains adjacent to the Treatment Plant, revealed a crossroad of pipes. One drain carrying waste from each site flowed at right angles into the Plant, whilst the third was meant to act as an overflow. Unfortunately the overflow drain was lower or had sunken lower thus allowing large quantities of waste to seep out of the site into the desert. This was evident by an outside wadi that contained vegetation. The simple solution was to correct the angle of the overflow drain in order to allow all waste to flow into the Plant. The overflow could still operate during the rare thunderstorms. The extra volume of recycled water necessitated a system of new piping and taps to be installed around the outer perimeter walls of the sites to carry the extra flow of water from the Treatment Plant. With the task complete it was possible to operate water sprinklers to all areas for a predetermined time period every evening. The end result was the complete transformation of the whole area with gardens with lawns, flowers, trees, tomatoes and other fruits flourishing. Over time the trees in turn invited a variety of birds, such as the weaver bird that weaved a basket type nest, and the bee eater. From my trips home I returned with small rose bushes for planting at the entrance to the sites, and slowly the sites developed in line with my vision.

There was a backlog in the maintenance of most aspects of accommodation and transportation. Whilst some of the Support Service multi-national work forces, referred to as TCNs (Third Country Nationals) were idle, others were inundated with a backlog of work. The introduction of a preventive maintenance system was required in order to avoid future backlogs. For equipment that should have regular check-ups, such as the air-conditioning units, I instructed that logs be kept and items tagged with the dates they were serviced. For vehicles, stickers were installed in each with the date or mileage recorded to indicate when the vehicle was due to be turned into the Auto Shop for its next service.

Drastic action was required to introduce the wholesale changes that I intended to bring about. Employees that were unprepared to co-operate with the reorganisation to raise the support standards were left with the option of having their employment terminated. In the early days more than twenty-five percent of my work forces took that option and had their employment terminated. By recommending a twenty percent increase in salaries for the remainder of the workforce I had a willingly team to successfully remove the backlogs in each department. The advantage of learning new skills was not lost on them; a plumber assisted in the Auto Shop, the air-conditioning staff assisted in the Sewerage Treatment. In this way, the staff learned to appreciate the long-term benefits of learning aspects of each others specialities, both to enhance their future employment prospects and for use about their own homes.

The catering department had its own separate problems to resolve. The GENA company employees, that we provided the overall support service for, had a contract entitlement of two meals per day, breakfast and evening meal. However many chose to cook their own meals in their villa kitchens, where the stoves were operated by gas cylinder. I decided to carry out evening visits around the sites to get some feedback from both the bachelors and families about their concerns regarding the services we were providing. During a visit to the catering department I questioned the late evening practice of closing all the kitchen windows, to let off smoke bombs. The purpose I learned was to eradicate the cockroach infestation problem. To solve the underlying cause of the problem I escorted the Catering Supervisor some distance from the building and removed a manhole cover to reveal an area that contained nests of roaches with young and eggs. With the introduction of regular cleaning of grease traps this proved an effective solution.

By inspecting the kitchen trash bins I was disturbed to discover the high degree of wastage. Quantities of unwanted single or two choices of sweet puddings, plus chicken carcasses and large bones containing meat had been discarded. Yet, soup was being provided from packets and cans. A variety of soups were introduced by using the surplus vegetables, chicken carcasses and bones with meat still on them, as outlined in a cookbook I presented to the Catering Supervisor. In addition I recommended that a larger choice of sweets be presented by using up small quantities of food that would be discarded. This allowed the cooks to use their imagination and reduce the amount of waste. The purchase of an ice cream machine that provided four different flavours proved popular. Another welcome major change to be introduced was to increase the number of meals on Thursdays and Fridays (the Arabic weekend) to three. This was achieved by having the cooks prepare a sufficient amount of food for a cold buffet for mid-day and evening meals. The dining room located next to the swimming pool made it convenient for the diners to enjoy meals by the pool. Two factors proved the changes cost effective; one was that the buffet required only two staff to operate the replenishing, cleaning and washing up. Secondly a number of families started to use the facility and were happy to pay for meals. To obtain feedback on the catering I introduced a suggestion and complaints book, in spite of the General Manager of Sites' advice that it would be a bad idea.

It proved a worthwhile experience to accompany the Catering Supervisor and a cook to the local market to purchase the weekly supply of fresh fruit and vegetables. Purchases were made with cash from my petty cash budget. The market was held in an open area where large truckloads of fresh produce were provided to supply the surrounding population. My morning venture proved to be more edifying that I had expected. Suddenly amid all the banter and bargaining a convoy of police cars escorting a van with grilled windows arrived. A whistle sounded, a hush descended on the crowd and as they were ushered forward, two policemen escorted a man from the van. The charge against the man was solemnly read out followed by the punishment to be administered. Soldiers on either side held the man's arms whilst the policeman administered a counted number of lashes across the man's thinly covered back. As the victim increasingly squirmed and cried, the punishment was administered with added gusto. I was distracted by the cook who was engaged in conversation with a detainee through the bars of the van, a fellow Philippine. He was crying in fear as he awaited his punishment. The cook managed to keep him distracted by having him relate the events that led to his present predicament. It appeared that he had been caught gambling and drinking when the authorities raided his accommodation. The second man, a local, was about to receive punishment for providing the alcohol, took his punishment without a flinch. The lashes in his case were administered lightly by comparison with the first offender.

The delivery of diesel fuel for the four generators and the supply of gas for vehicles further exemplified the poor lack of control in accounting. Each presented its own problems. Unannounced tankers arrived to replenish the underground fuel tanks for the Site's generators. The technicians signed the completed receipt for the quantity delivered. The problem was that there was no way to check the quantity delivered. I managed to establish that there were two underground tanks, one smaller than the other. No-one appeared to know or had until then, established the capacity of either tank. Once the capacity of each tank had been established I instructed the generator staff that future orders of fuel were to be requested by telephone only when a tank was empty. They were also furnished with a dipstick to enable them to keep a check on the tanks. By alternating the delivery between tanks it was possible to ascertain the correct quantity of fuel off-loaded to each tank. The same supplier of diesel fuel was also contracted to provide the gasoline and oil for company vehicles. Company personnel loaded up their vehicles at designated gas stations. Each vehicle was assigned a book from which the driver detached a ticket that he completed with the vehicle registration, date and quantity of fuel received. Once a month the total receipts for both the fuel for the generators and vehicles, together with the contractor's bill, were presented to my office to be checked before the bill was submitted to headquarters at Riyadh for payment. With one problem resolved another one reared its head. A random inspection of some gasoline tickets threw up a number of errors. Quantities of gas recorded on some of the tickets were well in excess of the capacity of the tank for the model of vehicle! A check of the vehicle's records for dates and quantities supplied revealed that alterations had been made to numbers, for example a figure 12 became 72. By issuing instructions to all drivers that future receipts should contain written quantities, in addition to the figures for the fuel received, I had hoped to remedy the problem. Not so, although it was now easier to spot the alterations at the next monthly check of receipts, the gas station attendant had not understood English! Needless to say the contractor was not best pleased with the drop in his future income.

An accumulation of large empty oil drums that lay about the Electrical Generation Plant were put to good use. Once cleaned and painted with white and red rings they proved ideal garbage containers, placed on the roadsides at intervals one per a number of villas. They provided an air of cleanliness about the sites and there were no longer scraps of paper and other debris blowing about.

Most of my waking hours were devoted to the task of transforming the sites into efficient and harmonious places for all their residents to live and relax in after working hours. To this end it was my responsibility to ensure that the provision of recreation facilities were of the best standard possible. This included the maintenance of the swimming pool, tennis and racket-ball courts. The buses that were used to transport the men to work at the Air Base, and for the children's school run, were also used for recreation purposes. This transport was used for trips to the seaside, shopping and to ferry expatriate nurses from the local hospital for weekend dances at our recreation centre. At the end of the evening I undertook the responsibility of driving the bus to ensure the girls arrived back at the hospital safely.

Monthly meetings were held at Headquarters in Riyadh, which all Site Superintendents attended. The purpose was to report and provide updates to the Director of FES on the various Support Services problems encountered by Programme Managers in the preceding month. We were also expected to account for any overspending in our budgets. My request for a suitable employee to be assigned to act as a deputy in my absence was granted. It was imperative that I had a reliable person to whom I could delegate my responsibilities and the Director of FES agreed with my choice of employee, the Riyadh Vehicle Maintenance Supervisor. The man was unhappy with being uprooted from his job and the change of location. To allay his fears I promised that if he still felt the same way in two weeks time he would be free to return to Riyadh. Within a week of working in such a favourable climate and the surrounding work environment he was very happy to remain. By December of 1982 he had assimilated sufficient knowledge of the duties and responsibilities and had become a suitable deputy. So it was that I confidently returned home for a month's vacation over the Christmas period. Each homecoming became more special as our family grew and on this occasion I met our fifth grandchild Kim, who had been born in the October.

During the rainy season a section of the perimeter wall collapsed. Work records revealed that it had become an almost annual occurrence during the thunderstorm season. The same section of wall was vulnerable to collapse due to the build-up of water force and pressure in that area. In order to discover the underlying causes of the flooding it was necessary to carry out a survey on foot of the external surrounding landscape. From a high vantage point on a rocky formation, the cause of the problem became visible ... the layout of a large formation of rocky outcrops created a natural narrowing funnel effect through which the water flowed. The simple solution was to hire a mechanical digger and create a long monsoon type drain some distance from the funnel to allow the water to seep through the scrubland and desert.

A big advantage of letting villas to different companies was the wide range of specialities they were engaged in. I was only too willing to welcome advice and assistance in resolving problems in which they had specialist knowledge. On this occasion we were fortunate to have a German construction firm newly accommodated on site. Their workforce was only too willing to reconstruct the wall in their own free time. I purchased the materials and agreed upon a price for the labour to undertake the work, at a more economical rate than if the work had been officially contracted out.

By the middle of the following year most of my objectives had been achieved. Empty bachelor and family accommodations had been renovated, furnished and leased to other companies. Such was the reputation we had acquired that I was forced to turn away applicants seeking accommodation. In addition to the wide range of recreational activities an increase in the quantity and variety of video programmes were ordered from the States for our studio. It was important for cultural reasons that our station signal was restricted to within the confines of the Sites.

Not surprisingly there were individuals who were not best pleased with some of the changes that were introduced. Many of the empty and partially empty villas that had been used to brew illicit alcohol for sale to fellow employees had been cleaned up and used as intended. The open and widespread practice could not be allowed to continue because of the danger to health and the risk to security. One individual, upset at the curtailment of his money-making sideline, vented his anger by scribbling profanities about every aspect of the service in the complaints and suggestion book. A very upset Catering Supervisor brought the matter to my attention. My reaction was not as he expected because I smiled: "There are three things to consider here, one he has an anger problem, two, his vocabulary is limited and finally he has abused his position and furnished proof with his signature."

Conducting negotiations with local

contractors proved to be a new cultural experience. The shaking of a hand that contained a wad of money was common practice. When offered a fistful of money I did not wish to appear offensive but politely refused and explained why it was not in our best interest to accept. One contractor who I had come to know talked to me about our custom of exchanging gifts during the season of good will, Christmas. How could I possibly refuse when he later presented me with a small neatly tied package and wished me a Happy Christmas? We shook hands and wished each other best wishes. Once he had left my office I hurriedly undid the package to find a shining new watch. I placed it in a drawer and proceeded to walk down the road only to pull up short and return to further inspect the gift. The sparkling watch was a black-faced gold and steel Rolex Oyster!

At our monthly staff meeting in Riyadh we were informed that the entire company contract was due for renewal by the middle of the year. With that in mind we were advised to curtail our spending pending the outcome of negotiations. A request from the GENA Programme Manger for the yearly replacement of his company car was met with my refusal. It was difficult to convince some company employees that there was a possibility the contract could be lost. It was a government military contract that had been awarded to the company from its inception. Some of those in company management could not envisage a rival taking over the contract.

Security was the one outstanding area of contention I still had to resolve. The guards manning the main entrance were old grey-streaked bearded local Bedouins who spent part of their days sitting and praying by a lone tree just outside the entrance to the site. Family members stopped and chatted as they passed by with their herd of goats. It would have been hard to guess their ages and I was informed that they did not keep records. Suffice to say that they shuffled rather than walked and spent much time asleep in the guard hut inside the gates. The planting of rose bushes and tomato plants gave a new purpose to their daily routine, as they appeared to enjoy watering them and derived the benefit of the fruit. The one remaining instruction I had yet to fulfil was to make the Gate Guards conversant with their duties. I was meant to publish adequate comprehensive instructions for them to follow in both English and Arabic. They could not read Arabic nor understand spoken English. Nonetheless I managed to convey the procedure required when checking visitors to the sites. The exercise proved a total failure because of the many complaints received from residents. Many had been chased away, threatened by the guards wielding their big sticks because they failed to produce a form of identity. They entered the Sites instead by climbing over the walls out of sight of the guards. The only option open to me was to issue them with a notice of termination of employment.

Shortly after sacking the Guards I received

instructions to report to the local Labour Court to answer a charge of unfair dismissal. The men had been advised to lodge a redress against the company. On the day of the proceedings, the promised company legal representative that was to act on my behalf failed to make an appearance. Fortunately I had taken an Arabic speaking member of my support staff with me to translate the proceedings. There was no requirement for the guards, or a representative to act in their defence to attend the hearing. It became clear to me through my interpreter that it was to defend the company's stand for dismissing the men. The Judge was patently acting in the defence of the man. He pointed out that after years of satisfactory employment it was only I who had found fault with them and this in the short time I had been in charge. During a break in the proceedings my interpreter warned me that the removal of my passport was being considered. The thought of not being able to leave the country to visit my wife and our newest granddaughter, Bernice was a powerful incentive to soften my approach to the problem. At the resumption of the proceedings I was shocked and surprised to be addressed in perfect English by the Judge. I could only assume by what followed that this fellow had visited Ireland and kissed the Blarney Stone.

"Come on now, you of all people being Irish should understand how these men feel. Imagine the threat they feel to their way of life, seeing tarmac roads being laid all over the land they roamed for centuries. These old Bedouins wish to live out their remaining days in their own traditional way. A rich and powerful company such as yours can surely not begrudge the small amount of money it costs in salaries to compensate these men for the changes you brought to the winter of their lives." In my urgency to bring about change I had failed to take account of the wider interests of these sons of the desert. With the lack of a legal advisor and the prospect of my passport being held I was only too willing to rescind the termination notice. The security problem was resolved by recruiting personnel from the Philippines. The new guards, dressed in smart blue uniforms, initially found it difficult to work alongside the old guards, but over time they drifted into a working arrangement. They conducted the guard duties whilst the old fellows carried on as normal: sleeping, praying and tending the flowers and tomato plants by the entrance.

In mid-1984 our Sites had a visit from the Company President, Vice President/Programme Director of GENA and the Director of FES. The purpose was to hold a meeting with all employees in the Dining Hall and to inform them of changes introduced to the Company's contract. The Saudi Government had decreed that in all future contracts they would be the major shareholder in the companies. Under these conditions the new company of Lockheed Arabia was initiated and had successfully secured the new contract. All company employees were thus affected by the winding down of Lockheed A/C International and with the transition of responsibilities to the new company. The implications for all employees, including my staff in the Support Service meant they were offered, or had to apply for new retention contracts.

With no intention of remaining in post with a new employer, my duties were then to arrange a smooth handover of the sites to the new incumbents. Most of the questions from the floor related to when and how new offers and conditions of employment would take effect. One known disgruntled employee who had already recorded his displeasure at the Support Service, questioned the likelihood of an improvement in services under the new management. Left to respond, I said: "As I will not be taking up employment with the new management, I am sure you will endeavour to acquaint them with any shortcomings as you have done with us."

At the conclusion of the meeting the President congratulated me for my work during my tenure. As we exited the building I pointed to the Complaints and Suggestion book that I had introduced which had proved an invaluable feedback tool in conducting our duties. He chose to peruse some of the entries. His outrage on seeing the scrawled obscene ranting of one entry came as no surprise. Turning to his Programme Director, he said: "I want this man to be suitably disciplined for bringing the Company and himself into disrepute." The author of the entry later visited my office to complain bitterly at me for allowing the President and his Programme Director to view his handiwork!

The new company chose to retain most of the GENA programme employees by offering them contracts. My Support Services Departments were retained including the laundry and houseboy services. During the early stages of the transition to the new contractor I made it clear that I had no intention of remaining in post. The transfer to the new man in charge went smoothly and as he had his own deputy, my second in command was happy to return with me to Headquarters in Riyadh. With our fully serviced, gas filled company vehicles we travelled the long sixteen-hour journey through the Empty Quarter to the warm dry heat of Riyadh. My thoughts were of home back in the arms of the love of my life, having at last achieved my long sought after dream. With our home fully paid for and sufficient funds to think of retiring, at long last I had control of my life to do as my wife and I wished.

At Headquarters I discovered that the Company Sites throughout the Kingdom were in a state of smooth transition to the new contractor, with the exception of the major ones located at Dhahran. These sites were unacceptable to the incoming contractor who chose to lease a nearby complex instead. The owner of the land and buildings on these sites, that were on a long-term lease to Lockheed was unwilling to accept the return of his property without a large sum in compensation for the run-down state of the property. Those expatriate employees who had accepted the offer of new employment contracts had already moved to the nearby complex run by their new management. The few men who had chosen to serve out the last weeks of their contract were housed in the small number of villas that were occupied. There were also a number of individuals from different companies renting some of the villas.

At a meeting with the Director of Facilities, Engineering and Services he proposed that I undertake the task of returning the Dhahran Sites to an acceptable standard which was to the owner's satisfaction. The challenge was tempting and I believe he knew I would think so. The call of my wife though was stronger and for me to undertake this task without her by my side was no longer a viable option. The Director offered to have my wife flown out to join me at Dhahran and confirmed that she would be offered employment commensurate with her capabilities. The urgency of my decision compelled me to contact Jean by telephone and explain the predicament I found myself in. Her willingness to join me in this new venture in Dhahran added an extra confidence to my ability to set about transforming those sites.

On Saturday, 17 November 1984 I was officially designated by letter to assume the duties and responsibilities of Site Superintendent, Dhahran. During my short stay in Riyadh I found my daily run to be much faster at sea level. The humid climate of Dhahran was similar to Bahrain where I had spent a year during earlier travels. The conditions of the Sites I had taken over were at least as badly run down as I was led to understand. After a quick assessment of the whole area I listed the actions required in order of urgency to return the accommodation and surrounding areas to a profitable operating standard. The main advantages this operation had over my previous one was that the supply of electrical power was on the national grid. The sewage drains operated in conjunction with the whole of the local area. We were also self-sufficient with water, which was supplied from a deep well on the property. Although the whole water system required some renovation. My multi-national work force consisted mainly of Koreans, Philippines and Asians.

Due to the low number of company resident employees on the sites, it was uneconomical to keep both the catering and laundry service operating. The majority of employees had accepted an offer of employment with the new incoming company and already moved to a new nearby complex. It was necessary to run down these services and compensate, by way of a financial allowance, the few that had remained behind to serve out their contract.

The water supply proved to have an inadequate pressure level to properly supply the villas furthest from the centre. Not unlike my previous experience the telltale signs of a major leak were visible. A clump of greenery existed in an area surrounded by desert. Excavation revealed a leaking water pipe that had been repaired with a piece of rubber inner tube wrapped round the pipe and tied with copper wire. In addition the outflow pipe from the main water tank was so badly corroded that it resembled a sieve. To carry out the repairs required scheduling the work to coincide with periods when the residents were away at work, because it meant shutting off the water for set periods of time.

With the instillation of a new submersible pump in the well and all other faulty pipes replaced the cleaning and renovation of the accommodation got underway. By the time Jean was due to join me the workforce were progressing well with the outlined objectives of transforming the site into an acceptable leasing complex.

The fleeting sight of Jean as she arrived at Dhahran Airport was an everlasting moment out of time. My concerns about her adjusting to the humid conditions vanished as I noticed the lack of effect it had on her. The ease with which she accepted the conditions reminded me of how well she had adjusted to similar climatic conditions years earlier in Singapore. With her by my side I was free to raise the invisible barrier that I maintained to the outside world. It was the beginning of the end of forging a long held dream. Together we would complete the final stage of my assignment before returning home to share our lives with our ever-increasing family. Little did I realise then, that she was the only person in whose company I could relax and feel at ease. With her I no longer had to be on my guard for fear of showing by word or deed of who I was or from whence I came. Few, if any could understand the lasting effects of having grown up in enclosed Institutions. She knew that I had chosen to deny that part of my life and would often unknowingly warn me of my ignorance of social niceties with a: "Please don't show me up." She would remark: "You're strange," whenever I failed to conform to convention, such as buying her a present on a whim. I never did quite understand waiting for 'special occasions'.

Her gentle, kind personality had an ongoing influence in my personal development. She had become my life's inspiration and filled me with the motivation to believe that everything was possible. Her presence also had an impact on my workforce. The duties of maintaining the accounting records, the petty cash and answering the telephone required little of her time. Often I would find her making tea for the cleaners and general staff in addition to helping two Korean staff with their English. Her efforts at getting them to pronounce the word 'fish' proved fruitless. After a number of attempts they all ended up in fits of laughter due to them repeating 'pish' it appeared the letter 'F' was not in their vocabulary. One Korean could not resist telling me: "Missy too good for you." Little was he aware that I would often question Jean and myself as to why she had chosen a stray like me. Her answer was always the same: "Because I love you."

As the programme of villa renovation progressed the demand to lease followed. One of the first companies to seek the lease of a number of villas was the Irish Electricity Supply Board (ESB). They had won a major contract with the local authorities. An aptly named Mr Power negotiated a long-term lease. It was immediately apparent to members of the company that I was Irish due to my still strong accent although I had not resided in the country since the 1940s. I came to recognise one fellow who unfailingly uttered the same words to my response to his telephone calls: "Is it yourself ?" For a split second the first time I had such a call, I looked to one side as if to question if it was me! When I mentioned this idiosyncrasy to one of his work colleagues, he told me his pat reply was: "No, it's me twin brother that was killed in the war." As a group they brought a degree of life and fun with their weekend parties to which Jean and I were always invited. I had however to be on my guard to deflect questions that arose about my Irish background. As good Catholics they were not to be denied their Sunday Mass and Jean and I were invited to join them. The practice of religion was strictly forbidden in the Kingdom, but I was to discover that these Irish folk had connections with Armco, the oil giants. Every Sunday morning Jean and I accepted their invitation to accompany them to Mass at the vast Armco complex. To enter the well guarded complex was to be transported to a suburban village in any part of the USA with its neat houses, lawns and clean sidewalks.

With most of the accommodation on our sites leased out, Jean and I had more time to visit the beach at weekends. I could only hope she had no regrets at not deciding to join me earlier in my quest to achieve my dream. She became friends with the many families and their children, and spent many an hour lazing by the swimming pool. We both enjoyed doting over a newborn child to the wife of one of our Philippine Security Guards. That may have been due to the fact that we had the news that a seventh grandchild had arrived back home. By then I was close to the completion of my assignment and we were both keen to meet the new addition to the family.

Jean accompanied me during my periodic visits to Riyadh to report on the Site's progress, where we were feted at some of the finest hotels in the city as guests of the Director of FES and his wife. Towards the end of 1985 I reported that all the work had been completed and that the whole complex was in a suitable condition to be handed back to the owners. At my final meeting, arrangements were made for both our inspectors and representatives of the owner to visit the sites to finalise the handover.

The owner's representative was unwilling to accept responsibility for the sites and insisted on minor details of work being carried out. Our inspectors were of the opinion that the sites were vastly improved as evident by the fully booked up accommodation. Prior to the programme of renovation the owners were initially in dispute with our company over a sum they required to compensate them for the state of neglect the sites were in. With no resolution to the dispute Jean and I visited Riyadh for the final time to attend a farewell party and make arrangements for our journey home. We returned to Dhahran to await receipt of my final salary settlement, air tickets and final instructions.

The final instruction was to hand the keys of the sites into the local Police Station. With that last act my working days were over, I was free to do as I wanted and had for the first time full control of my life. We were on our way home to live the dream in the home I had promised Jean all those years ago.

THE PAST RETURNS

We returned home to the house that Jean eight years earlier thought to be much too large. Now with our extended family of grandchildren, which grew over the years to a total of nine, there was more than enough room to accommodate them all for long or short stays. On weekends and school holidays the children would burst through the front door like a fresh breeze, shouting: "Hello Grand Paddy and Grand Paddywack." On one occasion our daughter was admonishing them for going into the cupboards seeking their favourite food. It thrilled me to see them feel so free "It's all right, this is home and they are very welcome."

It was early March 1986, our first year home, when a letter from the Ministry of Defence (MoD) landed on our hall floor. The envelope contained a letter stamped with a Manchester postcode and addressed to me at the MoD Personnel Management Centre, who had in turn forwarded it to me. The letter contained a telephone number at the top, with a short and to the point message that left me speechless as I handed it to Jean:

Dear Mr Rice,

This may come as a bit of a surprise, but I have traced you through the Ministry of Defence. What for you may be wondering!

Well, if you have a sister called Margaret who you have not seen for 37 years, and if you wish to be given her address, then please contact me at the above address. If you do not, then please return my letter. I have not told my mother about tracing you, as I wish it to be a nice surprise, so no harm will be done if you do not feel inclined to be reunited with the past.

Yours faithfully.

It was signed by the daughter, Margaret (Mrs)

I had no wish to be reminded of what should have been childhood but where I had instead spent fourteen years of my early life incarcerated in Industrial Schools. The shame and stigma I felt, forced me to deny that period of my life ever existed. The child Charlie I was once known as, no longer existed. For the remainder of my life, when the topics of childhood friends, family, school and social activities were raised in conversation, it was a signal for me to either change the subject or excuse myself. Now an unknown niece knew of my secret past. In 1947 I had run away from her mother and grandmother. They had misguidedly chosen to collect me on my ultimate disposal from Artane Industrial School. Had they just remembered a mislaid two-year-old child after fourteen years? I am never likely to learn all the true facts. Memories of spending a few short weeks, sharing one room in a wretched slum building in the Dublin of 1947, with a strange sister and her husband were best forgotten.

Jean managed to convince me that it was in our best interest to meet her new found sister-in-law and family. An evening phone call gave me ample time to mentally prepare for our visitor from the past. Arrangements were made to meet at our home over a long weekend. What our family members made of such a meeting I never knew. On a mild, early spring, Friday evening, full of curiosity we nervously awaited our visitors from Manchester. Waiting by the end of the driveway I became apprehensive and fearful about the meeting. The one memory path I had no wish to retread was that of my early years in Ireland.

'The Reunion'
Me, Margret, Jean, Joe, Marie with her daughter and Colleen with her children

Two cars rolled slowly to a halt at the end of the drive. From the cars alighted, my sister Margaret, her husband Joe and their daughter, whom they called Marie, with her small daughter. The years had been kind to Joe, as I had remembered him from our brief encounter in the distant past. The hardships of raising a family in the poorer part of Dublin City in the 1940s were visibly etched on Margaret's features. To have uprooted her family, including her mother, from Ireland to Manchester could not have been easy. Unlike her older sister's soft Irish brogue, Margaret's was flat with the discernable sound of a Manchester accent. Our meeting must have been a very emotional event for her. My formal handshake was ignored and I found myself in the sobbing embrace of a stranger. To hug or embrace was something I never managed to master with the exception of Jean or our children when they were young. For me it is an emotional expression of valued love shared. On that occasion I found it to be an unsettling and uncomfortable experience. Trapped in the embrace I stood motionless with my hands by my side, wanting to be freed. Had it been the hug of a male I would have immediately attempted to break free. How does one explain that first instinctively reciprocal embrace between Jean and I? It must have been love. That first special moment was as though the long-awaited loving touch of another human on an infant in a cot at Saint Patrick's, had awakened a dormant emotion called love.

In addition to her daughter and granddaughter, I learned that Margaret also had three sons; the eldest of which had emigrated to Australia. The family were visibly excited at meeting us and finding themselves at a large house deep in the countryside. Marie was the obvious spokesperson for the party and extremely protective towards her mother.

After a welcome meal Margaret, her daughter and I sat down in the main living room whilst Jean entertained Joe and his granddaughter. We both exchanged information about our respective families. Without any encouragement Margaret spoke freely about aspects of her early life. Painful though it was to recount parts of her story, I learned little of the causes for the initial break-up of the family. It was disturbing to note the bitterness and resentment that resonated from both Margaret and her daughter towards the memories of her older sister, Phyllis. Tears flowed with disjointed answers to my questions, with Marie comforting her mother all the while. The sum total of the information I had gleamed from our conversation was that: Margaret had been removed from the family home at about age six and placed in the custody of nuns in Dublin City. The grandmother and aunts on her father's side of the family gained custody of her sister Phyllis. As she understood it I, her baby brother, was placed in an orphanage for boys in the County of Kilkenny, some hundred miles from the family home. On learning that I had kept in contact with Phyllis since I had first tracked her down in 1948 they were surprised. The justifiable childhood anger and bitterness Margaret felt towards her older sister had understandably been passed on to her daughter. In an attempt to deflect that bitterness from Phyllis, it was necessary for Margaret to consider the facts as she had presented them and then to show them in their true perspective.

"Children always blame themselves or one another for breakdowns in the family. Phyllis would have suffered great emotional stress at the loss of both a brother and sister in one day. It may well have been, that as a nine year old she was considered the most suitable to be placed in the custody of the three older women. You would have viewed that at the time as her being favoured over you. There would also have been the real fear, if not the threat, that had she not been a 'good girl', she would like you have also been put away. You, by contrast were removed from your baby brother and older sister. All three children were removed from both parents. Yet 52 years on it is understandable that you should feel that it was so unfair for your sister to have been better treated. I was, and still am unaware of what happened. The only childhood memories I have are of life inside Institutions. As children neither of you were at fault for the pain you suffered. The fault lay with the adult's cruel actions, they were empowered to do as they considered best."

It proved helpful to have her daughter as an ally in supporting Margaret in coming to terms with the roots of the bitter feelings towards her sister. To suggest that her sister repaid the grandmother and unmarried aunts by caring for them in their old age was to illustrate an aspect of Phyllis' childhood. She had been 'a good girl' in carrying out her obligations by foregoing marriage until her late forties. It was important to remind Margaret that in spite of her painful experiences she had succeeded in raising a very close knit family of her own. After countless cups of tea with both of us during the long night and exhaustive conversation, the sun's rays begun to glint over the horizon heralding Saturday morning. It was with some relief that little interest or anything relating to my early life had surfaced during our meeting.

Late Sunday evening we waved our visitors goodbye with promises to keep in touch. There were the occasional visits in the following years, during which our pasts were never mentioned. It was on one of those visits that I learned that Margaret had brought her mother to live with her family until she finally passed away. Neither of her sons had fond words or memories to relate with regards to their grandmother.

Mid-summer of that same year we received the sad news of the sudden death of Phyllis' husband. They had been happily married for some twenty years. Jean and I were fortunate to be able to support and comfort Phyllis in her time of grief by attending the funeral and staying with her for some weeks. She and her husband had been supportive of us years earlier after the sudden death of our daughter.

That fact that Margaret had summoned up the courage to make contact with her sister a year or so after our first meetings proved a blessing to them both. I never did learn the details of how their initial reunion acted out. For a period of time there was no word from either sister. When I learned that Margaret and members of her family had accepted an invitation to visit Phyllis in Ireland it was a welcome surprise. The fact that they developed a close relationship was understandable. The bond created in childhood prior to the family being wrenched apart had stood the test of time. For a while the contact I had with Phyllis lessened. More in the hope of creating a bond plus the curiosity of discovering more about my family, I invited both of my sisters to spend a holiday at our home. It was to be the first time all three of us had been together since the break-up of the family over fifty years ago.

Our home environment proved an ideal place to relax and feel at ease with walks around the grounds, through the orchard and along the riverbank. On the final day of the visit we found ourselves sitting around the kitchen table after tea. The sisters and Jean chatted away about family matters in general whilst I listened. It was evident from the exchanges between the sisters that they had experienced happy periods as they reminisced about their childhood days. Wondering where I may have fitted into the picture I thoughtlessly interjected: "Margaret, did your mother ever mention me?" That brought a degree of tension and transformed the situation into a highly emotive one.

The word 'mother' written or spoken was one I avoided due to some inexplicable fear. Tears welled up in her eyes, "I don't want to talk about it. I have suffered enough," she blurted out, her body wracked with sobs. Phyllis rose to place a comforting arm around her sister: "We have all suffered, can we please let it be."

Margaret regained her composure and wiped her tears. Phyllis chose to divert discussions from the inevitably painful period of their lives when their world was shattered. "It does not do to dwell on the past, let bygones be bygones."

"Yes let's be a family now, we're too old to waste our remaining years raking over the past." It appeared that the sisters were in agreement. The thirst to discover the circumstances surrounding my detachment from the family remained unanswered. Then and there I had hoped to learn something from my past.

"My one wish as a child was to be part of a family. As I see it, family relationships are founded on some form of bonding. The only bonding experience I've had is with my wife and family. There is a need to build a bridge between us and that requires materials. Can or will you supply some materials to help build that bridge between us?" Margaret looked puzzled. "What sort of materials are you talking about?" At last I expected to learn a closely guarded secret surrounding the break-up of the family.

"I need, and want to know how I came to be abandoned and left to grow up in Institutions." Once again she was reduced to tears.

"I'm forever haunted by the scene of you, my baby brother, being wrenched away: the crying and screaming, you have no idea what hell I've been through." The soothing voice of Jean intervened:

"Let it be, love." She moved to console my sister. Consumed with a fuming rage I could not let up.

"I was confined to what I assumed to be an orphanage located more than a hundred miles away. At age ten, though I was then unaware of my date of birth, I was transferred back to Dublin to work and serve six years in the most notoriously cruel 'school' that was primarily used to contain delinquents boys. There I remained until my Ultimate Disposal at aged sixteen when both you and your mother arrived on the scene for the first time in my life."

"You have been successful in life, with a lovely family and home, so you see you came to no real hurt" my sister replied. I felt sudden stab of emotional amazement.

"To have grown up in State custody from infancy, not knowing who was responsible for my existence in the world is wrong. The damage is everlasting for a child to grow up without experiencing the touch of a comforting hand on their person." I had strayed into an area I had hoped to avoid and the words, 'you came to no hurt' brought a flicker of the vision of our daughter lying dead on the roadside. The rage subsided but try as I might I failed to stop the tears from bursting forth. Through blurred vision I saw Phyllis approach and place a hand on my shoulder. It felt as though she had touched an open wound, I winced and pulled away. I made my escape, dashed down the stairs and out of the house to be alone in the orchard. Jean joined me and the touch of her hand brought the required calming effect. In the cool autumn evening air we strolled slowly hand-in-hand with not a word spoken. It had been unwise to try and create a relationship with my sisters on much fractured foundations. My sisters would not, could not, bring themselves to reveal the answers to the many outstanding questions due to their individual traumatic experiences. More than two decades passed before I learned a little of the truth behind the reason for my incarceration.

At long last responsibility was accepted by the State for that sorry episode in its history, when shame and stigma became the inheritance of so many unfortunate Irish children. Unfortunately Margaret, like so many others, never lived to witness the public apology given on behalf of the country by the Prime Minister in May 1999:

"On behalf of the State and its citizens the government wishes to make a sincere and long overdue apology to the victims of childhood abuse and for our collective failure to intervene to detect their pain and come to their rescue. All children need love and security. Too many of our children were denied this love, care and security. Abuse ruined their childhood and has been an ever present part of their adult lives, reminding them of the time when they were helpless. I want to say to them that we believe that they were gravely wronged and that we must do all we can now to overcome the lasting effects of their ordeals."

The dream home in the countryside I had promised Jean in the early years of our marriage became a reality. With the renovations completed to both the main residence and cottage there was sufficient room for the children to spend holidays and weekends with us. Maintaining the land was a labour of love, cutting the grassy banks in the summer, mowing the grass on the flat and slopes

The grand children playing down by the river

and pruning the fruit trees. Each season brought its special beauty to be wondered at. Early snowdrops were followed by crocuses and dancing daffodils in the March winds. Cowslips, primroses and Michaelmas daisies adorned the banks by the orchard while bluebells blossomed in the sheltered space beneath the trees that bordered our land. The large pond by the river sprouted yellow lilies in the summer. The high-pitched clicking sound of shy moorhens could be heard as they trod daintily on the broad green leaves of the lilies that carpeted the pond. They nested and reared their young on the pond. Mallards and swans also built their nests along the riverbanks, whilst otters and mink could be spotted playing in the river. With the regular visits of fallow deer from the nearby woods came the problem of their damage to Jean's garden with their taste for roses, soft fruit and the fruit trees. The local Ranger was not surprised they visited our patch as he observed that I had created an ideal restaurant. We had unknowingly turned the place into a haven for a host of wild life that we were privileged to witness. There were stoats, weasels, and squirrels; in addition to rabbits and foxes that criss-crossed our land. Along by the riverbank it was possible to spot kingfishers whilst the fruit trees brought a wide variety of birds, in particular two colourful visitors, the green woodpecker and the greater spotted. The ground teemed with wildlife above and beneath, there were moles, voles, toads and grass snakes lazing in the sun or sheltering under rocks. The place was a wildlife wonderland too many creatures to instantly recall except for one I had heard of but never seen, a shrew, the beautiful small mouse-like creature with narrow face and long whiskers.

In the early 1990s we had the good fortune to have our daughter and her children stay with us while she sought a change of residence. The stay lasted a year and we were sad to see them leave. That very happy time flashed by but left a lasting cherished memory. Jean had returned to work to be reunited with her friends, whilst our daughter took the children to school each day and continued on to her work. The two-year-old Vicky and I enjoyed a new adventure each day. She helped me with my work about the property, sitting on my lap with her hands on the wheel of the small tractor while we cut the grass. Another morning she wondered what new task we were about to undertake: "Are we 'menting' today granddad?" She meant cementing; the small pointing trowel was best suited for her to 'help' me. She experimented by placing stones in the wheelbarrow of mortar and pretended to lay bricks. She loved the outdoors and wild life. As we walked along the riverbank one day I explained why swans were in pairs: "You see the one with the lump on its nose, that's the daddy one, it's called a Cob. The other one is known as a Pen, the mummy. Once they meet up they stay together for the rest of their lives." From the mouth of a child: "You mean they keep their promise."

When the family returned to live in the town all our extended family were never far away. They and their friends were drawn back to spend holidays, weekends and long summer evenings with us.

As our fortieth wedding anniversary approached I noticed that Jean had stopped playing her evening badminton. I accepted it in part with her retirement from work and took to an easier lifestyle. In the hope of cheering her up I arranged a surprise two-week anniversary vacation in Malta. We enjoyed our special day but I felt something of a change in Jean's demeanour. Her ever-present radiant glow appeared to slowly flicker on and off. I had failed to take heed of the early warning signs of things to come.

By the time our youngest granddaughter Vicky turned seven, her brothers had finished school, the eldest had joined the forces while the other was attending college. It was a time of change for all of us. Our daughter, her husband and their two girls spent a weekend with us prior to their departure to Abu Dhabi early on the first Monday of the year. Her husband had taken up a two-year employment contract. Early morning breakfast was taken in almost complete silence. Each of us had our own sadness to deal with. Jay, the seventeen year old, stayed with us to complete his studies. We each put on a brave face as the dreaded hour of parting neared knowing it would be six long months before we would meet again. By letter, two weeks later, we learned from our daughter how painful the parting had been for her. She wrote that it had been one of the hardest things she had ever done, even though she had left home years earlier in her life. In fact we had been parted years earlier, when Jean and I were in the Middle East: "But now, for the first time ever I feel alone, I know I have my husband and the two girls, but you have always been there for me. It is hard letting go when inside you don't really want to."

Shortly before our daughter and family were due home for a five-week vacation in the mid summer I received a telephone call from Phyllis. The normally lively, musical Irish voice was somewhat subdued. I delighted in teasing her with a mock Irish accent. "Is it your self, and what would you be after calling me for?"

"I'm sorry, it's Margaret, and she's dead." She sounded very distressed. I paused a moment to let the news sink in, and then struggled to find the right words.

"I'm sorry, it must be very painful for Joe, her husband and family." With my mind racing with confusion and frustration, I clumsily blurted:

"As you know I never really did get to know her, but I expect we should attend the funeral. She would have wished me to, as would her family. We will meet up at the funeral, it will be good to see you, especially now." She informed me that she had already booked the afternoon flight from Dublin to Manchester for the following day. Jean and I arranged to drive up on the day of the funeral and arrived just in time for the church service. We were strangers among my sister's extended family and many friends. As we departed the graveside with Marie by my side, I said: "I'm only sorry that I never really got to know your Mom." I was conscious of the time and effort she had put in years earlier to track me down.

"At least she got to meet you before she died, and that was her life-long wish fulfilled." Later in the evening at the gathering of the mourners, I questioned Marie's brother Patrick.

"Did your Mom ever reveal why we as a family were torn apart?"

"She never ceased asking that question but would not speak of the past."

"How in God's name could anyone have been so cruel as to inflict a lifetime of pain on innocent children?" He had become resigned to accepting the fact that it was part of Irish social history. "I expect to the social workers and others involved in the case it was just another day's work."

As we returned home I considered a chapter of my past had closed and that once again I could move on with our lives.

Another decade and more would pass before I would learn the true facts of the appalling life long devastating affects the State/Church had wrought on each member of the family. Given due consideration to these facts, there was very compelling reasons why my sisters were unable to recount the very traumatic events visited on them as children. Prior to my birth Phyllis the eldest girl, was age four and Margaret aged two would have witnessed the birth of a baby brother. Two years later another boy was born. The girls would also experience the trauma of the deaths of both brothers. Some twenty months later, my arrival must have been seen as a prayer answered and a welcome blessing of 'third time lucky'. Their lives were not to be so blessed. Two years after my birth, the girls then aged eight and six, were to suffer due to the irreconcilable break-up of their parents' marriage. Shortly after the break-up, both Margaret and I were charged in Dublin DC on 9th February 1934, with receiving alms and sentenced to serve nine and fourteen years respectively in separate Industrial Schools. It was the intension of the authorities that I should have no further contact with any family members and to that end they succeeded. Not surprisingly when we did eventually meet we were total strangers.

The vacation of our daughter and her family from Abu Dhabi was really special. I had taught the children that the most precious commodity we all have is time. We know not how much we have: it can't be made, or bought. I intended to spend as much time as possible in their company, especially with Vicky, whom I felt had taken a part of me with her on her departure. Although the stay measured in days was long enough, from early July to mid August, the time appeared to vanish like a fistful of sand.

Vicky and I were inseparable. Each morning

she would pad around the house barefooted whistling or singing, much to the annoyance of her mother, who would remark: "She's a morning person." Vicky would ask of me "are we going down to the field?" Try stopping me! It was like opening a door on each new day, to enter the world of a child and see anew the beauty around us. With a keen eye she would spot where the deer, rabbit, foxes and otter had visited over night. As we walked along the river bank with its swans and mallards in the river and moorhens in the pond we would sing some of the silly songs I had taught her, like:

I climbed up the door. I opened the stairs, said my pyjamas, and got into my prayers.
I switched off the bed and crawled into the light and all because she kissed me good night.
On the baby's knuckle or the baby's knee, where will the baby's dimple be? Baby's cheek or baby's chin, seems to me it-ill be a sin, if it's always covered by a safety pin, where will the dimple be?

On the first day of their vacation we went into the next field where sheep were grazing in the morning sunlight. The smallest sheep of the lot came up to Vicky. It differed from all the others. It was very tame, had long pointed ears, a narrow small mouth and a heavy straight coat. Vicky named it Pixie as it followed her around the field. Each day we would visit Pixie to feed her leaves from the elder and willow trees by a stream, and small apples from the orchard. Each morning Pixie could be seen pacing up and down on the other side of the fence anxious to meet her new friend Vicky to be fed apples. We would lift the wire fence to let her graze separately on lush well maintained lawns. Vicky even managed to get Pixie to climb a low-lying willow tree by a stream. A strange sight indeed, to see a sheep and young girl sitting up a tree!

One evening as I looked from the landing window, three stories up, I saw someone sitting by the riverbank. With the use of binoculars I could see it was Vicky, Louisa (an older cousin) and Pixie who sat chatting in the tall grass by the riverbank, a peaceful picture. We spent time picking wild flowers for her Mom or sat on the tractor mowing the grass. I watched her uncontainable excitement when we found a small vole in a pile of newly mown grass. We lay on the newly mown land in the afternoon sun. We chatted beneath a rich blue sky, adorned with wisps of white leisurely clouds reluctant to vacate the silky splendour of their blue bed. High above a small dark shadow of a buzzard sailed across the sky on wings that never seem to fly. These scenes were to be wondered at and loved.

In the slanting sun Vicky took my hand: "Come on old man" and before I kissed her goodnight she remarked: "Granddad, you told us that all grown-ups are only children who have grown old." We spent a portion of our time that cannot be unspent. Its pictures and colours are confined to the library of the mind, for future viewing. That was a special summer.

On Sundays we renewed our ritual lunch, with all the family, followed by a walk along the narrow winding road to visit the lakes and feed the deer and pot-bellied pigs in an enclosure. Along the way we picked ripening wild cherries at the roadside. All too soon it was once again time for their return to Abu Dhabi and it would be Christmas before we would meet again. Prior to her departure Colleen expressed concerns about her Mom's apparent loss of interest in her appearance and other everyday matters. I assured her that it was probably due to changes with age and her retirement. I reassured her that I would take good care of her. We maintained contact by telephone and letter. The letters from seven-year-old Vicky showed signs of a freedom of mind and spirit. There was the constant reference to her pet Pixie enquiring as to how it was and that I should pet Pixie for her. One statement she made resonated with me many years later. She corrected me when I wrote inadvertently about her coming to 'our house' by reminding me that I had always maintained that our home was her home and that she would always consider it to be so. She complained to her Mum: "It's not fair Jay (her older brother) is allowed to stay at home and not me, I want to go home." Later in life as a nineteen year old she remarked: "If ever I have enough money I'd buy our home." Home truly is where the heart is.

Jean waving goodbye to Colleen and the family

Six months later, while home on vacation Colleen extracted a promise that I would ensure her Mom visited her doctor for a check-up. As a result of the visit the doctor prescribed anti-depressant medication. By the time Colleen's husband's eighteen-month tour in Abu Dhabi was completed and the family returned home I had become acutely aware that something inexplicable was happening to Jean. She started to have erratic short-term memory loss, such as forgetting where she had left her cigarette pack. Colleen confided that her Mom had asked her advice about medication for her memory and insisted that I accompany Jean to the doctors. Jean's doctor referred her to a specialist to conduct tests. Little was I aware that our visit to the specialist, a Psychologist, was the prelude to a long torturous journey.

My heart sank as I watched Jean attempt to master simple memory and co-ordination tests set by the specialist. She watched intensely as the doctor demonstrated the simple task of clapping his hands alternating between flat hands and the open and closed fist. Her attempt clearly demonstrated her co-ordination was almost non-existent. Coached to repeat word for word a simple three-line address a number of times, she was then distracted for a short period by questions about her general health. When asked to recall the address her memory failed her. The end result of our visit was a recommendation for an MRI scan. At our follow-up visit to the specialist he explained the results of the scan: "I'm very sorry to tell you it is Alzheimer's." Displaying the x-ray he pointed to a dark area: "As you can see it is pretty well advanced."

LEARNING ABOUT ALZHEIMER'S

Unannounced and unnoticed this life stealing disease invaded our lives. In spite of the prompts from our daughter for her Mom to visit her doctor, I either chose to ignore or was blind to the early signs of an illness that would herald the beginning of the end of life as we had known it.

It was akin to being presented with a box containing the pieces of a large jigsaw. The picture on the cover was of a white canvas background. Large numbers of pieces were damaged from trying different methods to force them to engage. Many are the days I have cursed the lack of even the shadow of a picture, or the provision of written instructions to assist with the jigsaw.

I now find it ironic that over the years Jean would often remark: "You're strange." Considering my background it should come as no surprise that logic should prevail over emotion when it came to reasoning a solution to a problem. In the absence of nurture, nature ruled. On occasion Jean had expressed concern at hearing me musing to myself over a problem:

"They'll take you away; you're always talking to yourself."

"I'm just thinking aloud, sure there's no-one about."

"Yes, but I've also heard you argue."

"Ah go on with ya, I'm only working out the pros and cons of something I'm trying to solve. Should I lose what you may call an argument, it'll be time to take me away."

It was years before I came to understand some of the torment she must have been put through. Knowing her as I did over forty years her fears of being 'put away' were so very real that she attempted to conceal the early onset of Alzheimer's. As a child she may well have noticed people vanish from her community and thereafter, family members speaking of them only in whispers. At best they would say of them that they 'were not right in the head' or 'had gone funny'. Like most parents and grandparents she would not wish to be a worry or burden to her family.

I had failed to fully appreciate her sense of insecurity as she constantly attempted to 'go home'. To her 'home,' was a place she constantly attempted to retreat to. A childhood home where she understood all her troubles would vanish once in the safety and warmth of her family with Mum and Dad to care for her. Numerous times she attempted the hundreds of miles journey 'home'. When she intimated she was about to go home I offered to accompany her. Along the road hand-in-hand we strolled conversing all the while. Unaware the topic of conversation had slowly changed along the way. As she tired I distracted her with the offer of a drink as we turned for home and thoughts of the childhood home had vanished for the moment.

During the following year or so small warning signs of what lay ahead began to appear. Life carried on as normal except for intermittent incidents such as when she helped me make tea one day. I had placed a tea bag in each cup then attended to other matters while the kettle boiled. As I poured the water on to the tea bags I was surprised to find that I was pouring boiling coffee from the kettle! She developed a habit of picking what I believed to be imaginary specks of dirt from the carpets and family member's clothes. New manifestations of this strange disease appeared and then disappeared for a time, but kept returning within a shorter time span. Finally they would return as a permanent part of the jigsaw. Caregivers often refer to this phenomenon as 'having good and bad days.'

Without noticing I found myself taking on the cleaning, washing and shopping full-time. While shopping at the supermarket she tended to wander off and become lost and scared. It was not unlike shopping with a young child. On one occasion I went searching for her only to find her chatting with three staff members. They appeared to be enjoying themselves:

"There you are." I smiled with some relief.

"You can sod off" she told me, to which the girls laughed and asked if I was her husband.

It was wonderful to see her demonstrate a sense of control of the situation and to show that she was "the boss" in the relationship! On another occasion we returned home from the supermarket to find that she had left her handbag in the ladies toilet. It was late evening by the time I discovered the missing bag and phoned to enquire about it. We were fortunate that a message left for the cleaners recorded that the bag had been handed in to the local police station. It was a relief to find everything in her handbag was safely accounted for. For years we followed a ritual every weekend of grocery shopping followed by a walk with the youngest of our grandchildren to our favorite café in town. There we had coffee, cream buns and soft drinks. Jean would also give each of them £1. The practice continued until the last of the grandchildren had reached an age where they were no longer regularly sleeping over at our home. Keri, the eldest of our son's girls and by then a qualified hairdresser, would pop by the café to see her Nan. The children were unaware that Jean was ill and I was conscious that she did not wish them to know. There was an incident when she offered Keri a £1 coin. Keri looked at me with embarrassment and gently refused the coin. As Jean held it out I nodded my head urging Keri with a look to accept the offer. On another Saturday at the café Jean excused herself to go to the toilet. After a considerable length of time she failed to return. A request to a member of staff to search the toilet proved negative. I panicked and dashed on to the street in search of her only to find her talking to our daughter-in-law who happened by.

The warning from our eldest grandson Lea, forced an unpalatable decision to be made:

"Granddad, Nan is a danger to herself and others on the road, she should not drive." From that moment on I planned to undertake all the driving with a promise to spoil her by being her personal chauffeur, being at her beck and call to drive her home when she wished. I came to regret being careless with the safety of the car keys. Circumstances forced another painful decision to be made; to take control of all of Jean's affairs before it was too late. I passionately believed in Jean's independence and freedom, and had encouraged her to control her own affairs. A situation arrived that left little option but to speedily apply for Power of Attorney. There were many heartbreaking incidents to endure along the way. One that tugged at my heartstrings occurred during the process of organizing her personal clothing and effects. She possessed a number of handbags, many pairs of high-heeled shoes and clothing that was no longer safe for her to wear.

Among the contents of the handbags were small bundles of notes squirreled away. In total they amounted to around eight hundred pounds! She sat next to me on the bed and I was filled with sadness. For a moment words failed me as I held back the tears: "What was this lot for?" With a sad expressionless look, she replied: "I don't know." Filled with sadness I held her close knowing that whatever her intention had been it could no longer be fulfilled. The short-term memory losses may have been the reason she had not deposited the money in her own bank account, or our joint account.

Her short-term memory loss proved to be a positive factor in relation to her smoking habit. A number of times she mislaid her cigarette packet and replaced it with a fresh pack. An arrangement was reached whereby I would retain the pack and issue her with two or three cigarettes at a time. The practice appeared to work well for a while but her smoking became somewhat erratic. A stage was reached where she appeared to smoke far fewer cigarettes than the number I gave her. The mystery was solved when I thought I had found her mislaid reading glasses case. The glasses were missing and in their place was a case full of cigarettes! Here was another part of the jigsaw complete; the smoking habit had vanished without me noticing.

Jean's urge to go home grew stronger which meant that I had to keep her close by at all times. I could ill afford to spend long periods looking for her while engaged in household chores and the maintenance of the land. The local Alzheimer's Society was the logical place to call to seek advice. The lady in charge invited us to a party that was being held at the Society's building. We parked the car and walked the half mile to the building in silence. I was taken completely unaware by Jean's adamant refusal to enter the building. The lady in charge of the centre approached to invite us in, but Jean was resolute: "No, I'm not going in there." I had never witnessed such fear in her before. The lady gently coaxed Jean to join her in the garden for a cup of tea. With that the tension subsided as we sat down to drink and chat. It was a day centre where caregivers placed loved ones for a period respite. We departed the centre by walking straight through the building and proceeded to walk the half mile back to the car. Out of sight of the building I was very concerned at what I had witnessed:

"What was all that fuss about, refusing to go into the building? I have never seen you so upset and frightened."

"You're trying to put me away." I was shocked and saddened and for a spilt second, my mind conjured up a picture of the stray she had taken on all those years ago sitting patiently on the lawn outside. I owed her more than I could repay.

"I could never do that to you, how could I cope without you?" A heavy silence fell over us as we made our way home.

Once a month an appointment with the Psychologist was arranged to monitor Jean's progress and we were assigned a male nurse to visit our home on a monthly basis.

Life carried on as normal as possible by sticking to a routine. The older grandchildren moved on with their lives and we entered a new stage in ours.

As we walked around town on a Saturday I failed to recognize two young women approaching us: "Hello Nan, Granddad." They were our son's younger daughters and had grown into attractive young women. They were unaware of the seriousness of Jean's condition. My attempt to illustrate their Nan's short-term memory loss was foiled.

"I've lost track of the days, do you know what day is it today sweetheart?" She smiled:

"Yes, but I'm not telling you, you should remember."

The monthly visits to our local Psychologist came to an unexpected end when he was transferred to another city. He provided us with a telephone number and the new location for future appointments. The due date of our monthly appointment passed without notification and when I called the new practice to enquiry about an appointment for the month of October I was met with a surprise. The receptionist took our details: "I'm sorry there are no appointments arranged for your wife." I questioned why not: "Your wife is sixty-five and we don't see patients over that age." It was early October and Jean's birthday was on the seventh.

New warnings and incidents of what this disease had in store for us would suddenly appear then vanish for a while just as suddenly. The first sign of incontinence was the message deposited on the bedroom carpet. When I asked Jean why she had 'messed' on the carpet, she told me: "That wasn't me, it was the dog!" In sheer disbelief, I said: "We don't have a dog." "It was

Queenie." That was the name of her family dog when she was a teenager.

With the helpful advice of the male nurse I learned when to fit incontinence pads during the day and night. Coming to terms at first with toileting her was extremely frustrating and initially I became short tempered. On one occasion I helped Jean on to the toilet and wiped her bottom when she told me she was finished. I next helped her onto the bidet to wash and hose her, only to find she had defecated in the water before I turned on the sprinkler. Once again she denied that it was her mess. That was a steep learning curve and I soon managed to adjust to a new daily routine.

Other incidents and situations were sprung upon me but unnoticed I had drifted into the caring role without realizing it. To see her lose her ability to function normally served to make me love and protect her all the more. She began hallucinating as the experts called it. I chose to explain it by her seeing objects and people that I could not. Standing on the landing by the window on the top stairs, three stories up, she asked: "What are those two girls down there doing on our land?" I asked her to describe them. She clearly described their clothing and hair colour. When I asked about their footwear, she told me: "They're stood in the long grass, I can't see their feet." As far as I was concerned the girls were there though I could not see them.

Why can it not be that visions of places and

people from an earlier time enter her confused mind? Her childhood memories were clear enough for her to keep attempting to return 'home.' If she is in the area of her childhood is it not reasonable to assume she can see in her mind, people and places there? It may equally be that she is at times sleepwalking or daydreaming. One summer afternoon we sat looking across the landscape. She was staring vacantly into the distance, and so I asked: "What are you looking at?" "A big woolly sheepdog" she told me. When I asked where it was, she indicated the skyline. At first glance I could see no sign of a dog. I could only see the skyline covered in a broken line of trees. Try as I might to enter her world I still failed to grasp that she was regressing to childhood. Sat there watching the trees in the distance, suddenly I could visualize the distinct form of a large sheepdog taking shape formed by some trees! The visions in her world I chose to accept had logical explanation. As a lone child in my first Institution I retreated into my own world and had my make-believe friend.

On one of our weekend outings we bumped into our teenage grandson Marc, our son's boy: "Granddad, you remember you promised that we were always welcome to stay with you and Nan? Well can I come and stay with you." "Of course you can." I agreed without hesitation, our home was the family home. There was no thought given to the added burden I was taking on. Fortunately he went to work daily and had a wing of the house to himself and room for friends to visit. The wing had three bedrooms, two bathrooms, kitchen and large sitting room plus a separate central heating system. Nonetheless I cooked, cleaned, washed and ironed his clothes.

Once on our weekly visits to town we walked linking arms together when suddenly I felt Jean lean on me as she slipped to the ground. It was a warning I learned to heed of what to expect in the future. There were no more walks or visits to the cafe in town. From then on our weekly visits were restricted to the supermarket. As anticipated she did not fall again for a period of time, but other signs of her failing special awareness began to show. She required assistance when descending stairs. By inviting her to lean on me, I would place a hand under her thigh and place her leg on each step of the descent. One Sunday as I was preparing lunch she stood on top of the landing waiting for my assistance. She was fearful as she stood looking down and refused my offer of help:

"Please relax and stay up there while I get on with preparing the lunch. I'll help you down in a few moments." Back in the kitchen as I was busy preparing the meal, I heard a sound and as I turned to look, there she was beside me!

After a considerable period of time Jean was assigned a new lady Psychologist to monitor her case on a monthly basis. The numerous offers to avail ourselves of a period of respite, I finally accepted. The doctor arranged for us to inspect the centre. The place was a small, friendly, well-staffed safe unit and a trial respite of one week was arranged. There after a second week's advanced booking was arranged for two months later. On my regular visits to the secure centre Jean appeared to have settled in well. Her respite period offered the chance to catch up on a backlog of tasks about the property such as grass cutting and collecting the fruit. It was my misfortune to injury my back while trying to lift a loaded trailer. Though painful I carried on working and caring till it became impossible to cope without medication. The injury caused muscle wastage in one leg, so an appointment was arranged for me to be examined by a Consultant at the General Orthopedic Clinic at the local hospital. His prognosis was that it was probable that I required an operation. There were more visits during the waiting period when treatment and medication was prescribed. In addition I set myself a daily routine of exercises to strengthen my back and legs. An operation was no longer required but further appointments over the next year were made to monitor the progression.

Jean's attempts to return 'home' still persisted. I considered her to be safe so long as she remained in the vicinity of the property and land. With both the large wooden doors closed at one end of the drive and gates at the top end, I misjudged her determination to go 'home.' There was an occasion that she managed to find her way on to the highway without my noticing. Finding her missing I checked all the rooms in the house, the land and outbuildings. Driving slowly along the narrow country road I turned on to the main highway, soon I spotted her making her way along the grass verge. She was wearing a slipper and a Wellington boot! As I pulled up beside her, I asked:

"Where are you making for sweetheart?" "Home" she replied.

"Where is home?" I asked and to my amazement she recited full details of her 'home.' "14 Whitwell Terrace, St. Helens, West Auckland. "

That had been her home as a child, some forty-five years earlier where she had first invited me as her young man to meet her family. Her childhood home and all others had been demolished and replaced with new housing more than thirty years earlier! It was another lesson to be taken on board with still more to come. The next lesson I should have learned earlier. She left my side for a moment while I was preparing Sunday lunch. I thought she was not too far away, but after about twenty minutes I became concerned but decided she could not have gone far. My concern proved misplaced, as she entered the kitchen looking pleased:

"Where have you been?" I asked.

"Buying a cake." I thought, 'fine, this should be interesting':

"May I see your cake?" She left for a moment and returned with a large chocolate cake! Somehow she had gotten hold of the car keys and driven a round trip of around twenty miles to the supermarket. Any other morning there would have been more traffic for her to contend with. It never did occur to me to question where she got the money to pay for it. I was just greatly relieved that she was safe.

To travel down the strange Alzheimer's road was a painful enough journey without having the ghosts of my past unleashed. It happened by accident that we were watching the evening news on TV when the dreaded name Artane was mentioned. The item referred to a public apology made by the Irish Prime Minister on behalf of the government to the men (then children) who had suffered abuse, while in State custody. The apology was decades late in forthcoming but at least now there was an admission, which meant at last I could, with thousands of others, make my voice heard. The blanket of fear and shame was raised to let some light shine on the darker side of Irish Social history, relating to treatment of those children held in State custody.

Christmas of 2000 and the millennium passed us by with little or no celebrations as it was necessary to maintain a normal routine. The party our grandson held with friends he had over to welcome in the New Year went unnoticed because it was restricted to his area. We saw little of Marc other than my delivering his meals before and after his day's work. He was unaware of the degree to which his Nan's condition had deteriorated. He joined us on our daily morning walk on the land one weekend. On our return we were about fifty meters from the steps leading up to the house when Jean stopped and pointed to the foot of the steps:

"What are those two men doing there?" I looked to Marc:

"Shall we go and ask them?" He smiled, tilted his head and pursed his lips as though to whistle. By the time we reached the steps it seemed they had vanished.

On reflection it may have been a wise decision to have her eyes checked, but checks such as that and hearing become lost whilst concentrating on all the problems Alzheimer's brings. About this stage trees appeared to become an attraction to Jean. On our walks of all the trees on the land, and there were many, she would climb a small bank to embrace one of the sixteen tall Scots Pines.

By spring Marc decided it was time to move on with his life, which resulted in my workload being lightened somewhat.

During the warm weather I kept a close eye on Jean as I worked on the land by moving her chair to a convenient spot as I moved about, felling a tree or planting vegetables. The peace of the countryside allowed time to reflect. As I observed the circles on the stump of a newly felled tree I was reminded of Jean's illness. The rings represent the age of the tree, not unlike our age. The inner circles, the first years were deeper and bolder in colour whilst the outer ones were lighter and appeared to fade with time.

In August I received my follow-up

appointment at the local Orthopaedic Clinic. The results showed I had made good progress due to my exercise routine and light jogging around the land. The one outstanding problem I was experiencing was synovial fluid on a knee that responded well to an injection. There was to be another visit to the hospital and when I received information on the treatment proposed I was greatly concerned. The title read: Facet Joint Injection. It went on to describe the procedure of how a steroid would be injected into the spine. After reading through the complete treatment I became more determined to complete my own recovery. On 3 September I presented myself for the treatment.

Whilst waiting for the Radiologist the nurse reassured me the procedure was painless. The Radiologist asked where my pain was located: "There is no pain." I told him.

"Can you touch your toes?" I duly did.

"There is no point in giving you an injection. It would be like giving you

paracetamol when you don't have a headache."

The Consultant at an earlier appointment had remarked into his Dictaphone; "This man has problems coming to terms with aging." It was just as well I had as it was to prove of enormous benefit over the following years.

Towards the end of September if I thought our lives could not get any worse I was sadly mistaken. It was a warm sunny afternoon, perfect weather to sit outdoors. Jean was wearing slacks and a light white cardigan as I put a cushion on her chair and placed a glass with a cold drink on the table for her. I ensured the doors at the end of the drive were closed before leaving her to attend to some work on the land. On my return, no more than half an hour later, she was no longer there nor was the glass or cushion. Suspecting she had gone indoors I hurried upstairs but she was nowhere to be seen. A quick dash around all the rooms proved negative. I ran around the buildings, cottage and land in search of her but to no avail. A check of the road either side of our property showed no sign of her. By then I was in a panic as I checked around the pond and along the riverbank then returned to the house to phone our daughter. She lived about eight miles away and I asked her to check the road as she came over to help in the search, whilst I waited at home in case Jean turned up. Colleen had not sighted her Mom on her journey over. There was only one option left; to contact the police. They arrived with a tracker dog and we each arranged to search designated areas. Colleen drove slowly along the narrow winding roads; I rechecked the building while the police with the dog searched the surrounding area. It was late evening when the suggestion of a helicopter search was mooted. Just then Colleen and a policeman accompanied a very subdued looking Jean to the house. She had walked no more than two hundred yards from our house and turned towards a neighbour's house high in the woods. She left their driveway and climbed into woodland. In the gathering dusk Colleen had spotted her white cardigan as she held on to a tree for dear life.

Only days later life was never to be the same again we were about to be put through what could best be described as a living hell. The first of October 2001 was a mild damp morning with intermittent hazy rain. I was about to accompany Jean on our morning walk at about nine thirty:

"I think it best if you wait inside the door, the grass is wet and not safe underfoot, I won't be long." I had walked halfway down the bank towards the river when I heard a thud and a groan. Jean was laying face down where she had fallen forward. As I rushed to her side I knew she was hurt by the sound of her soft whimper. She held her right arm as I supported her back to the house; up the steps, and then along the spiral staircase into a sitting room and sat her down. A hurried phone call brought her doctor who in turn arranged for an ambulance to take Jean to hospital. The diagnosis was a broken arm and dislocated shoulder for which she received a painkilling injection. I assisted her into the ambulance and followed on in the car. We waited for about a half an hour to be attended to. Our strict routine dictated that I take Jean to the toilet to change her pad. I walked her along a corridor in search of a female nurse to assist with toileting and to provide a clean pad. It would appear that our absence from the waiting room had been spotted by a male nurse who came running after us, followed by a doctor:

"Where do you think you are taking her?"

"I'm taking her to the toilet." The doctor appeared agitated; "That can wait, she requires treatment now." Once I explained her situation they left us to get on with our business. Back in the waiting room the male nurse began to explain to Jean what was about to happen. He failed to grasp the fact that I was acting on my wife's behalf and was adamant that I was not allowed to enter the operating theatre.

The raised voices attracted the attention of the theatre doctor as I insisted on accompanying the trolley taking Jean to the theatre. He signalled for quiet as he pointed in my direction: "He is the only person I want in here, the rest of you leave." Turning to me, he said "Calm your wife and reassure her that she will be OK while I put her under." He placed the mask over her face while I held her left hand and spoke soothingly. It was eleven o'clock in the evening by the time I saw Jean safely bedded in a large mixed ward.

The following morning I received a call from the hospital informing me that Jean would not speak or eat for the staff: "That should come as no surprise she is in a mixed ward amidst a bunch of strangers." Immediate arrangements were made to have her transferred nearer home at a local cottage hospital. During my daily visits I noticed a marked change in her appearance, she was either asleep or lying listless in a chair. The sight of her thus prompted me to request staff members to encourage her to walk about the ward. They said they were walking her although the only time I witnessed movement was seeing two of them supporting her to the toilet. To see her sitting alone in the patient's area at the end of the ward, was fast asleep with urine dripping from her chair onto the floor caused me great concern. My concerns about her mobility grew daily to such a degree that I decided to help her from her chair and walk her. When a member of staff intervened I was adamant that if they were not going to exercise her then I was. The sister in charge admonished me and summoned a doctor to have a word with me. My concern was that my wife might not be able to walk by the time she was discharged. Though she was being moved about in a wheelchair he assured me that she would be able to walk. After almost three weeks the injuries to her arm and shoulder had healed sufficient to have physiotherapy. I watched as a nurse moved Jean's arm up and down to exercise the ball and socket joint in the shoulder. Jean grimaced with pain as she reached her left hand in an attempt to remove the girl's hand from hers. The nurse stopped: "I'm sorry does that hurt?" Almost in tears she could not answer and so I said:

"You're hurting her hand, the one injured in the fall that took the full impact."

"There is nothing in the notes about an injured hand." The injury had gone unnoticed in spite of her hand being curled, swollen and unable to open. Hurried arrangements were made to have the hand x-rayed.

Respite had been scheduled some months prior to her accident and after a month in hospital she was transferred to the well run small respite centre. I waited at the centre to see her settled in. My worst fears were confirmed when she arrived in a wheelchair. A bigger bombshell exploded when the matron reviewed the accompanying paperwork, she looked very upset:

"Why has your wife been given Temazepan? She is a very quiet gentle person."

"I don't know, what is that?"

"It's a sedative to keep patients calm,"

"You're upset",

"I'm bloody furious! just wait till I have words with those responsible."

The following morning I phoned the hospital to complain about my wife being sedated during her stay. In addition, I said that if they insisted that they had been walking her then it must have been sleepwalking. Our daughter accompanied me on visits to the homely centre and supported her Mom as we walked around the small sitting room. Though we both knew that she would never walk again we left it unsaid. Jean received no treatment for her injured hand, which by then had set into a curled up position.

At the end of Jean's two-week stay, the Respite Centre made an appointment at the local hospital's Orthopaedic Outpatient Department. The attending Consultant was the same person that had attended to my earlier back problem. The ambulance personnel handed Jean over to me in one of their wheelchairs. At that moment it dawned on me that my caretaking situation had totally changed, I now had to manage an immobile loved one without the use of a wheelchair. The ambulance personnel had told me that it was my problem to get her home. As I wheeled her into the treatment room my stress and agitation was plain for the medical staff to see. The ambulance personnel were unconcerned as to how I got her home. The Consultant thought he had allayed my fears by arranging an ambulance to return her home. He proceeded to examine Jean's arm and shoulder and pronounced they were healing fine. An inspection of her injured hand revealed that it was not possible to fully open it out. In his view it was not worth operating to straighten the fingers but arranged an x-ray to determine the damage. My sense of agitation at the predicament I found myself in did not go unnoticed:

"When I get her home I have no idea how I'm meant to manage washing, changing and moving her about to put her to bed."

The Consultant wished to test her mobility and together we raised her from the wheelchair. However, she was incapable of standing unaided and was notably in pain. He was astounded to discover that no arrangements had been made by the Social Services for Jean's homecoming. He instructed one member of staff to fetch the physiotherapist to discuss treatment for her hand. Another staff member was ordered to contact the Social Services to provide assistance that evening and the following morning with preparing Jean for bed and raising her for breakfast. The ambulance crew members were the same crew that had arrived some six weeks earlier to deliver her to the hospital after her accident. As they lifted her into the house one remarked how she had walked on to the ambulance and in to the hospital back then.

The service provided by the Social Services proved totally unsatisfactory. The arrangements were suited to their discretion, by the help arriving at seven o'clock in the evening to make Jean ready for bed. The morning help arrived at nine o'clock. This meant she would be in bed for a total of fourteen hours. After a sleepless night I had her up by seven o'clock; washed, dressed and fed. The house was not best suited for the type of care Jean now required. To move her within and outside the house I hired a wheelchair from the Red Cross. One of the sitting rooms on the second floor of our split level house served as a bedroom for her. In addition to the converted bedroom we were restricted to a sitting room, dining room and kitchen in which to move about.

The spiral staircase to the ground floor restricted our only exit to the garage, and driveway. The only option was to negotiate the difficult one step down and two up form the front of the house through the gate to the sidewalk.

At night time I chose to put her to bed just before I retired for the night. The sudden change in my care giving role took its toll on me. The fact that she could no longer feed herself and was unable to communicate properly I found distressing and stressful. Due to a lack of sleep and worry I found the caring more difficult to cope with.

One morning after I had washed, fed and set Jean down to watch TV, I went down stairs and outside for a breath of fresh air. Suddenly a number of people descended from nowhere, two nurses came down the drive, others made their way to the front door. To the best of my recollection there was a social worker, doctor, a carer's support reprehensive and our daughter. Much later it transpired that our daughter was rightly concerned for my health. Too drained and worn out I went along with the decisions they arrived at. It was agreed that a hastily arranged two week stay at a local Nursing Home would be of benefit to us both.

I prepared Jean for her move and packed her bags. Colleen, the doctor and I sat in the kitchen for a long period waiting for the transport to take her to the Nursing Home. Filled with a deep sadness I was lost for words not knowing what the future held.

Once again I was back and forth journeying to visit Jean, we were being torn apart by this evil illness. Her injured hand had begun to swell and was held in a fist which resulted in the moist skin peeling. She was prescribed pain killing medication for the constant pain. In the second week of her stay a meeting was called to arrange a package of care to suit her needs when she returned home.

The package never came to fruition as Colleen explained, 'the carers were incapable of operating the proposed plan due to her Mum's injuries'. It was too big a risk as they were insufficiently qualified to cope.

There was only one option left, one I never expected nor wished to consider: 'to place Jean in a Nursing Home'. Without our daughter's support it is impossible to envisage how I acceded to accept the arrangements of 'putting her away'. Parted from my soul mate, the love of my life and my purpose for living I felt like a child lost. I also had to live with the guilt of having broken my promise.

OUT OF SIGHT BUT IN MIND

Though I did not know it then, it was a dreadful mistake to have placed Jean in a Nursing Home. Like many of those that suffer with dementia, I also came to view the places as prisons, a place to end their days with no chance of reprieve. These places are generally located many miles from the local communities, as were the institutions for destitute and orphan children decades earlier. Within living memory similar centres were used for patients with mental disorders like dementia. The unspoken social principle of 'out of sight, out of mind' then prevailed. At least lessons were learned in relation to retaining vulnerable children in Institutions where nurturing and love were lacking.

Half-heartedly I tagged along with our daughter to visit a number of Nursing Homes. The place of our choice was heavy with an old air and wore a weak look as though it too was ill. With cowardice in my heart I handed over money to Colleen to open an account for her to manage the monthly charges. We returned to Colleen's home with the move agreed. Slowly the realisation of what I had done sank in. With tears in my eyes I held my arms open seeking comfort and support. We fell into each other's embrace and sobbed. I had placed the control of Jean's care from then on in the hands of strangers.

The thirty mile round trip to visit the Nursing Home became a daily routine. Fearful to learn what the future held in store for us, Colleen and I researched the progressive stages of the disease. From the information available it was possible to deduce that Jean was in stage seven, the final stage. The separation caused both of our health's to suffer as long as she remained in the Home. During daily visits a feeling of us being torn apart by the staff added to my frustration. Without knocking a member of staff ducked her head around the door of Jean's room to disapprove of my attending to her toenails: "You're not supposed to be cutting her nails" she said and then vanished.

In normal circumstances Jean would have hushed me whenever a protest in my mind rushed forward to the tip of my tongue. In a rage I dashed from the room into the cold December air to cool off. My distress had not gone unnoticed by other members of staff who reported the incident. The following morning I was invited to the Matron's office where the offending staff member was instructed to offer an apology for her behaviour. The words were spoken but there was little contrition in the voice. Thereafter I referred to her as 'the old bat' because of her long period of service there. The same woman addressed Jean in a manner I found irritating:

"Good morning Jeanie and how are we today?"

"Her name is not Jeanie, its Jean." I said and the 'bat' left the room:
"You don't like her, do you?" I asked Jean and through her facial expression and head movement, I read a firm no.

In spite of having all her clothing, including her socks, sewn with nametags like a school child, I constantly found Jean dressed in other resident's clothing. On one occasion she was wearing tights, something that as far as I could recall, she had never worn. In a fury I removed them and threw them from her room. As her condition deteriorated I spent longer periods at the 'Home'. Initially a physiotherapist attended to her injured hand a number of days a week. To keep the hand open, a light alloy frame was strapped over her hand to hold it open. With the progression of the illness the physiotherapist disappeared from the scene without notice. The longer I spent at the place the more frustrated and irritable I became with the whole aspect of continual carelessness.

The place was unsuitable for the number of dementia patients among a host of others. There was Bert with his cheerful greeting: "Ello mate", engaging me with a query: "Have you seen my wife?" Gently I informed him she had passed away twenty years earlier. When he asked; "Where do I pay for my meal?" I told him, "Bert, you have paid for everything, this is a holiday home and the staff are here to look after you."

There were a number of ladies trying to wriggle out of dementia though having nothing to do to pass God's good time. There was Iris who shared a room with Nester. When she was not wandering the corridors and in and out of Jean's room seeking her son, I would take her hand and guide her to her room. Other times I took Iris along the corridor as she repeated a telephone number and then sit her by the front door to wait for the son that never came. Her daughter-in-law was her only visitor. Nester, was a kindly old lady with thinning hair and no teeth. In a high pitched voice she kept repeating: "I can't see, I can't see." A request to a staff member to attend to her was met with: "A lot of them shout for no reason." A number did shout but was there a hidden reason? The lady in the room opposite to Jean kept shouting out letters that appeared to form the words of an address. Intent on resolving Nester's problem I entered her room and it was easy to discover why she was unable to see, her glasses were clouded with a little talcum powder. With her glasses rinsed and dried at the sink she was thankful, in addition I gave her one of the soft-centred chocolates I kept for her. When I looked into her eyes and peeled away the withering years it was possible to imagine the beautiful young girl within. This lovely woman appeared to have no visitors. The most distressing memory I am left with in relation to Nester is seeing her trying to remove her incontinence pad whilst sat in a chair, by pulling it forward and upward. I reported the matter to staff members and no urgent action was taken. Shortly afterwards the sound of rushing feet to and fro was heard. When silence descended I popped my head into Nester's room and was shocked to see her face and arm badly damaged. Instinctively I put my arms around her and found it hard to hold back tears.

One never tired of listening to May relate the story of how she helped to raise her brothers and sisters on the family farm after her Dad was killed in the First World War. There was also the old man that banged on the floor to attract attention. Spending so much time there I became an accepted part of the establishment. So it came as no surprise that a staff member summoned my help to solve the mystery of the old man's floor banging. He had a problem with changing channels on his TV. She had switched the set on but could not change channels using the remote control. It was possible to change the channels from the TV, but as he was bedridden he required the use of the remote control. A quick check revealed the remote control contained no batteries!

In the beginning I meekly followed the daily procedures such as vacating the room when requested to allow the staff to change Jean's pad. I waited in the corridor until invited back into her room. At meal times I wheeled her to the dining room and assisted with her feeding. In the spring of the year I took her for walks along the nearby country roads. On our return from one such outing we sat in the yard of the home. A member of staff approached:

"Has your wife had her lunch?" Unwilling to reply, I said instead:

"Why do you ask?" She failed to grasp the significance of my asking that question. Some time later I found out that my concerns were well founded. Jean had not had a change of pad from after lunchtime until teatime at five o'clock. A staff member approached:

"Will you be staying to feed her tea in her room or in the dining room?"
"I'll feed her here, but first could you please arrange to change her pad as it has not been changed since lunchtime." The change was duly completed with a promise to deliver her meal. After some considerable time lapse with no food in sight I made my way to the dining room to find it empty. The one person in the kitchen cleaning down was the same one that had promised to supply the meal. My presence came as a shock: "Oh, I'm so sorry I forgot all about you, I'll rustle up something right away."

The one service that was never overlooked was the ladies weekly hairdressing sessions that were included in the monthly costs of the 'guests' stay. The place seemed to whisper cynically of profits for management and unfeeling methods of care. Staff turnover was high and pay was low. They did however eat well in their staff dining room. When I asked a staff member, if she would wish a member of her family or herself to end up here? Her two-word answer summed it up appropriately: "No way."

Jean holding our great grand daughter Ellie

By the late summer of 2002 Jean weighed less than six stone and I was becoming more frustrated with the standard of her care. My mood towards the staff became belligerent. No longer was I prepared to leave the room when the staff arrived to change her pad: "Could you please leave?" "No." "But you must." When I questioned why I could no longer be present, they said: "It's for her dignity." I exploded: "What the hell are you talking about, dignity? How would you like complete strangers to strip you naked and wipe your bottom? Who do you think has been changing, washing and feeding her long before she came here? We have been married for forty-seven years and all you people have been doing is separating us. It is not going to happen, I'm staying." The girl stormed from the room but returned moments later to join her co-worker to perform their duty in my presence. What I then witnessed will remain forever etched in my mind. They held Jean by her upper arms and as they lowered her pants, her left foot rested on her toes. The skin hung loose on her ribs; there were no longer buttocks just limp hanging flesh. The left buttock was black with what looked like a leathery texture. The right one was a raw blue and red hue. Shocked and upset I left to seek an explanation from the duty nurse. The young male nurse explained it away as part of the progression of the disease. The reason she could not bear weight on her left foot was due to a deep pressure sore on the heel.

Without consciously being aware of it I had taken to spending up to eight hours a day with Jean and had taken on the tasks of changing, washing and feeding her. She was bedridden by then and I became deeply concerned about her state of mind. One morning I arrived to find her looking very upset with me. From what little communication we had, she believed I had been absent for a long period of time. Though I explained that I had been home only to sleep and for a quick change of clothes, I knew she was incapable of understanding. The daily journeys to and fro took their toll on my health and as a result I was prescribed anti-depressant, sleeping, and irritable bowel syndrome medication. I was no longer capable of maintaining the land, cleaning the house and devoting my time to caring for Jean. My first priority was to her, without Jean I had nothing. During the Christmas period staff numbers were reduced due to the vacation. Members of the cleaning staff were co-opted to assist in the dining room. One of these offered Jean a hot cup of tea. I was prompted to point out the danger of presenting her with a warm drink when she could not hold a cup. In an earlier incident she had been scalded on the thigh when attempting to hold a hot drink. The staff member took my warning as a rebuke, was upset and reported me. When the Sister in charge raised the subject with me I offered my apologies to the woman, but she made it quite plain that she was not interested in an apology. After another stressful day I returned home to a restless, sleepless night. In the early hours I remembered the story of a sleepless wife whose tossing and turning husband kept her awake. In the story Lyn asked her husband:

"Nick, what's worrying you?"

"I owe John £500 and I don't have the money to pay him." John and Mary were friends who lived opposite to them. Lyn jumped out of bed, pulled back the drapes, opened the window and called to Mary across the street:

"What do you want at this hour of the morning?"

"Nick owes your husband some money which he can't afford to pay him." She closed the window, pulled the drapes and jumped into bed.

"Now we can sleep, it's no longer your problem"

Even knowing that the staff on duty may well have been asleep during the early hours, I chose to telephone the Home to relieve my frustration and anger.

The fact that Iris had become bedridden within three months of her arrival and passed away within six months had a sobering effect. I recalled her initial stays at the Home were introductory overnights, before her final residency. I had gotten to know and like her as she wandered the corridors of the home trying to break out of the mist of Alzheimer's. She was a widow and her only visitor was her daughter-in-law.

Jean became so depressed and dejected that I felt compelled to ask the question her body language exuded: "Have you given up?" My heart sank with the nod of yes. I reached forward and held her frail body close as I held back bitter tears and begged her to hold on to the promise that she was coming home. It was necessary to keep repeating that promise to reassure her. To jog what memories she may still have retained, I played family videos of the previous twenty years. Regular outings to our daughter's home helped to break up the monotony of her daily Nursing Home routine.

The dream of the home I had long wished for and promised Jean had ended and our house was up for sale. Our grandchildren had once run free there and such happy childhood memories are still retained there. However without Jean the place was dead and my heart ached to be with my beloved Jean. By late November the sale and purchase of properties were completed. The move was a harrowing experience, so much so I could not bring myself to be involved in the purchase of the new house. It fell to Colleen and her eldest daughter to select a new property for us. Unfortunately, although the new house was situated only minutes from a supermarket and doctor's surgery, it was not fit for the purpose we required. The property required double-glazing throughout and for the dining room to be converted into a bedroom. A conservatory was a requirement to house the dining room furniture and an outside balcony built with decking as I intended to wheel Jean on to it in the summer time. The ground floor bathroom was altered to contain a shower, small hand basin, toilet and floor fitted with non-slip tiles plus a water drain. Finally a ramp was necessary by the front entrance to accommodate wheelchair access. With a price and contract dates negotiated and agreed, work started in mid-December with a completion date of late March 2003.

I had taken to using my video camera to record Jean's condition both inside and outside the Nursing home. It was made clear that the use of the camera was not welcome in the Home; nonetheless I filmed. In the proceeding twenty years I had filmed the family get together at Christmas time and that year was no exception. Though I had moved into our new house while the renovation work was in progress, I took Jean to our daughter's family home for Christmas lunch. It is still painful to view the recording of her condition as it was then. We returned to the Nursing Home in the late evening in time for her bedtime. Only one member of staff was available to ready her for bed. She was one of the pleasant caring girls and I was happy to assist her prepare Jean for bed. I recall another girl refer to her as the coloured girl. It made me smile and the black girl laughed as I corrected: "She's not coloured, are you? We are the coloured ones, with grey and blue eyes, blond, red and white hair and pale, red and tan skin plus some of us with blue or red noses."

As soon as the renovations on the house got underway I advised the Matron of my intention to remove my wife from the Home. She informed me that a meeting would have to be arranged to discuss the matter. Said meeting was arranged for 28 January 2003. It included representatives of Social Services, senior management of the Home and Matron. Colleen came along to both support and dissuade any criticism I might have expressed about the standard of care. The proceedings were of little interest, my sole concern lay with the removal of Jean from the home and to devote whatever time we had to care for her. When asked why I wanted to remove my wife I replied that I considered a Nursing home was not a suitable place for victims of Alzheimer's. Every effort should be made to support and keep them in their own homes. Failing that they should be housed in small units within their local communities. The Social Services representative retorted:

"If everyone held your views there would be no need for Nursing Homes." "That would be a very good thing" I replied. Colleen must have felt somewhat embarrassed: "You'll have to forgive Dad; he lives in a make-believe world." The outcome of the meeting resulted in me being granted permission to take Jean home on 3 April. As Colleen and I walked free of the Home my step was lighter and her remark came as a surprise:

"Dad they are pleased to be rid of you and Mom."

"What makes you say that?" I asked.

"Oh come on Dad, you were spending everyday there and noticed everything that went on and you have not been the most diplomatic of people."

"I really don't care; I'm thrilled knowing we will be together again."

In addition to her failing speech, rigidity had started to set in, which resulted in Jean's hands turning in at the wrists. A daily soak of her injured right hand in warm water and a gentle massage whilst opening the hand, helped ease the stiffness. With a little ingenuity I made a crepe bandaged-covered, sausage-shaped sponge to place in her hand. This helped to absorb moisture and allowed for light exercise of her hand. Jean's feet and ankles had become so swollen to the extent that it became impossible to fit her footwear any longer. I had disposed of all her shoes with the exception of a new pair of leather boots; kept in the hope of her wearing them at a future date. Until such time, an outsize pair of ankle high slippers kept her feet warm plus thick woollen bed socks. Confident with the decision I had taken to bring her home I became more assertive about her care. When I questioned the duty nurse about the different medications being administered, she suggested that I consult the doctor. Jean had hidden some of the capsules in her mouth and spit them out. The summoned doctor lauded what he considered my devotion to my wife:

"I understand that you spend many hours here taking care of your wife, you are doing a wonderful job." I thought such a comment strange:

"No it's not." He looked surprised:

"Why do you say that?" Without thinking words spilled forth:

"Don't dogs look after their pups?" There was a moment's silence.

He went on to explain the various medications being administered for the different symptoms she suffered. Up to that date and even later on, we were never made aware, nor were any medications prescribed that may have been available for treatment of her illness namely, Alzheimer's.

The best description I could conjure up for her loss of memory was to liken the memory bank to a box of tissues. The last tissue in is the first one out, the purpose for only some being removed may be possible to recall. By the time one reached the first tissues in the box, they are the last out, by which time the purpose for removing the tissues has been forgotten. So it was with Jean when she was due home only her first sub-conscious memories remained; those of an infant.

There was no time to consider the full ramifications of the decision to remove Jean from the Nursing Home. All I was concerned about was regaining control of our lives; living together again without outside interference. My thoughts were concentrated on hurrying the contractor to complete the renovation of the property to make it fit for purpose. My days were spent with Jean and the dark evenings spent purchasing drapes, blinds, a wheelchair, commode and other equipment for the task ahead.

My life regained a purpose and whenever I had a goal to achieve I refused to be deflected from my driven path. My natural instincts took over and I found myself back to my lifetime routine of running. I ran every night before bedtime. My spirits rose at the prospect of no longer having to waste valuable time parted from my love. In running I was both mentally and physically stimulated. Running allows the mind to contemplate solutions to complex problems and to place them in the right context.

With the work near completion I arranged to take Jean home for over-night stays on 18th and 25th March. The stays went well and were followed by a three-night (Friday to Monday) weekend stay. The visits were arranged with the Nursing Home's approval. Much later I came to the realisation that for the five days she was in my care, I had not been provided with any of the medications they were administering to Jean on a daily basis. On reflection I also thought it strange that no-one had considered inspecting our house to ensure that it was fit for purpose. Could it be that our daughter was correct when she remarked that they were happy to be rid of us?

Our lady Psychologist was the one person that kept a keen interest in our case. Her suggestion that I may be trying to keep Jean alive for my sake prompted a question of my motives. When asked why I was so adamant on removing Jean from the Home, she was appalled at my initial reasoning. In trying to see a Nursing Home through the eyes of a patient suffering from Alzheimer's, I saw them as prisons. How can a young person know the fear of a seventy-year-old plus person upon being separated from a loved one and their home? Add the confusion of the disease, a strange environment with strange different men and women tending to your most personal needs would make any sane person agitated and aggressive. The Nursing Home's answer to these problems is to sedate the patient. In fairness to the Psychologist she sought my alternative to Nursing Homes. My ideal would be to keep people in their own homes and pay a large enough tax-free sum to the main carer to compensate for loss of earnings and enable them to pay for help. Her response was that it would prove too costly. Most of these Homes are miles from the nearest towns. The cost in transportation of staff, food, maintenance and visits of relatives on long roundtrips adds to already over crowded roads. Relatives were paying vast sums of money towards the keep of their loved ones in these places and they are run for profit. As for the people who cannot be cared for in their own home, with a little imagination small units within their own communities could be created. Friends and relatives could pop in to help in the unit and wheel them around their area. It was suggested that I was too forwarded thinking and that change takes time. There was a time when institutions for orphans and destitute children were maintained at arms length from the rest of society, as were mental institutions. The time is long overdue to confront all forms of dementia with openness, to end the out of sight, out of mind attitude.

As the day of our reunion approached my fears vanished and with them my anger and frustration at being parted from my soul mate. No longer was I prepared to accept interference in our relationship or lives. For the foreseeable future I intended to be consulted and involved in any medical attention Jean required.

THE GIFT OF TIME

Whilst in the process of transferring Jean and her personal effects to the car for the journey home I was apprehensive and fearful about my ability to cope with the task that lay ahead. Prior to our departure from the Nursing Home I was handed a large paper bag containing the various medications used in her treatment. These I in turn handed over to the doctor at the local surgery, informing her that I viewed them as serving no useful purpose. However, I was strongly advised to retain one bottle of paracetamol suspension to use to relieve pain. My first priority was to ensure that each of Jean's injuries was treated to relieve and eliminate her pain. Once that objective was achieved I intended that there would be no repetition of the underlying causes of her injuries.

Our daughter was awaiting us as we entered our house. I felt a stab of anger to find that on removing Jean's slippers, true to Nursing Home form, she was wearing socks with the name of another patient emblazoned across the toes! With a voice tight and hard, I vowed: "I'm going to take back control of our lives and do this on my own. I don't want strangers interfering."

The offending socks I later handed over to the lady Psychologist who had maintained a close interest in our case as it unfolded over the years.

On the first day of April 2003 the fact that we were reunited and had once again regained control of our lives, appeared to allay my fears and worries. As I retired that first night, I looked forward to our first day together and was not disappointed. Although Jean was very ill, her facial expression conveyed better than any words the sense of safety she felt at last. There and then I knew that I had done the right thing in bringing her home. During the first visit from her doctor I was strongly advised not to force feed Jean, as her doctor pointed out I would not care to be force fed. Our daughter Colleen concurred with that advice and begged that I not attempt to feed her. From my perspective Jean had regressed to a stage of infancy and was very ill. As such, she required the tender loving care only a trusted loved one could give to encourage her to eat and drink. She may, or may not have known who I was, but she could see, hear and feel. Her emotional senses appeared more acute. She knew the sound of my voice and we could communicate through touch, sound and sense as we looked into each other's eyes. After forty-seven and half years of marriage she was my soul mate, who therefore was better placed for her to turn to when she needed tender loving care?

It came as no surprise that Jean had difficulty eating; she could no longer swallow with ease. She had lost weight; she now weighed less than six stone and could no longer support her head, which resulted in it falling back. She had spent long periods breathing through an open mouth the questionable dry centrally heated air of the Nursing Home. In addition, the lack of a daily tooth brushing routine had led to the inevitable consequences of the development of an oral thrush infection. She was bedridden and rigidity had set in. It was illogical to continue to lay her on her back. A simple remedy to this problem was to place Jean on her side in the foetal position and to rest her head on a pillow angled to rest up against the headboard. To maintain her head in the downward position a second pillow was placed behind the end of the first one to support her head in a downward position. With her chin thus it became possible for her to breathe through her nose. By rotating her position at regular intervals during the day it reduced the risk of further pressure sores. The constant use of a swab moistened in water and mouthwash helped to clean her gums and teeth and stem the infection. To initially improve the quality of her breath I placed fast dissolving thin slivers of mints on her tongue.

There was little time to consider the enormity of the task I had undertaken; so much to do in too short a day. There were advantages I already had over many other caregivers. Aged 72, I still retained a clear mental picture of the time era and place where Jean had spent her childhood years and had now mentally regressed to. To enter her world I talked of the early 1950s, her teenage years when we first met. I conjured up a clear mental picture of what her school days and childhood activities might have been like. There was no question as to my physical ability to stay the course because I continued to maintain my life-long fitness regime. Through trial and error I settled into a daily routine, rising at 04.40hours every morning to complete a three and a half mile run before breakfast. Because there was little time to dwell on the final outcome I had embarked on a labour of love and chose to confront my fears as the unknown. Had I chosen to live in fear I would have lost control. The answer was to continue learning and accept each unknown part of journey we travelled together. There was no cure and as with all of us the journey's end is the same. Like many caregivers there was a time when I may well have questioned "Why us?" The answer is simple; why not me, there are countless paths to our final goal, the problem being that we perceive them as happening to 'other people'.

Our daughter often remarked that I lived in a 'make believe' world. In my early life I had found mental comfort in that world. To appreciate each moment in time I was granted in the company of my love I adopted a mindset with the analogy of a small craft. With some effort I endeavoured to remain in our craft I named 'NOW' as we navigated the river of life and avoided disembarking into the future. Should my mind have drifted from the NOW (that moment in time) I hurriedly re-embarked. Each precious moment she survived, powered my love for her. There were bound to be storms and fast currents mingled with peaceful periods along the journey. She became my beautiful baby and I cared for her accordingly. She was a very good baby and slept safely through the night and for long periods during the day. Initially during sleep periods I was kept busy with the washing, ironing, cleaning, cooking and all household chores. It was a very humbling experience to enact the day-to-day life chores that she had endured as part of the daily norm during our long years of marriage.

The pressure sores, the turned in hands and oral thrush were not the only indicators of the shortcomings in the system she endured whilst in the care of others. Her face was pitted with blackheads; her nails were unkempt and grimy, plus her ears and her teeth had gone unchecked. It was easy to rectify some of the problems with skin cleansing cream, baby wipes for her bottom, talcum powder, cotton buds to clean her ears and nostrils plus regular changes of the most suited pads to soak up maximum urine to avoid leakage and soreness. Special pads with Velcro strip fasteners for overnight use proved very beneficial.

Medical help was initially available to Jean in the form of daily home visits by a nurse to monitor her condition and to maintain a diary recording her treatment. The initial entries appropriately describe Jean's health upon her return home, as follows:

Past Medical History: Alzheimer's – does not speak, unable to self-care.

Present Medical History: unwell – for palliative care.

Social History: Husband wanted Jean home to care for her.

Client Handling Risk Assessment Scores: Weight 1 (below 7 stone)

Mobility: 10 (Totally dependent/Comatose)

Additional risks: 5 + 4

Total score: 20. Scores 0 to 8 = low risk. 9 to 15 = Medium Risks. 16 plus   = High Risk.

A week after her return home an Occupational Therapist arrived to carry out an assessment. She observed as I transferred Jean from the bed to a low armchair: "You're very gentle with her." Why would I not be, in her state?

A similar remark made by the Matron at the Nursing Home I had found equally incomprehensible: "You really do take the vow, 'in sickness and health' seriously."

The Occupational Therapist ordered a hoist to help move Jean, plus a Kirton high chair that could be wheeled about. This and other equipment arrived by the end of the month. The hoist I placed in the garage, as Jean was far too light to require a hoist. An early extract from the diary recording our situation noted that: "Husband is continuing to care for Jean who is totally dependant upon him. He needs support, is reluctant to ask for help at present, although his daughter feels he needs help."

Contrary to the doctor's advice I persisted in feeding Jean three times a day, opening her mouth and feeding spoonfuls of liquefied food that took time for her to swallow. Through trial and error I learned to wait till she swallowed before offering the next spoonful. When I waited too long she refused to open her mouth, it was as though she had forgotten I was feeding her. There were occasions when it took up to two hours to complete a meal. I discovered there was a rhythm to feeding. With the use of pineapple juice drinks I hoped to improve her oral hygiene. The original children's plastic beaker as used in the Nursing Home proved totally unsuitable; it was impossible to monitor her thirst. A more suitable container I discovered was a wide rim diameter glass that provided an all round view as she drank.

During the two months that followed, in spite of some set backs Jean appeared to be making a slow overall improvement in relation to her physical condition. For a short period her body shook with tremors, which I interpreted as part of the illness. Without warning they vanished as quickly as they had appeared. On reflection I concluded that they must have been related to the withdrawal symptoms from the concoction of drugs administered at the Nursing Home. It became possible to lift Jean onto the commode and wheel her to the bathroom to attend to her ablutions. By mid-June she relapsed into a pyrexia (feverish) state and on the morning of 13th June 2003, during her ablutions she began bleeding profusely from her bottom. I summoned her doctor who arranged for an ambulance to have her rushed to hospital. Before accompanying Jean in the ambulance to A&E I contacted our daughter to meet us at the hospital.   Colleen and I waited anxiously in the hospital corridor for news of Jean's condition. After a long wait we were informed that an x-ray had been conducted which had failed to reveal the problem. It was further explained that to operate was not an option as she was unlikely to recover from an anaesthetic. Jean was hooked up to a drip and oxygen mask and placed in a communal ward with patients recovering from operations. As I returned home I was left with the impression by the staff that I should 'let nature take its course.' On my first visit the attending nurse informed me that Jean had refused all food and drink. The fact that she was unable to speak or feed herself never arose. When I requested some food to feed her I was furnished with a yogurt and teaspoon. The nurse was somewhat taken aback at the ease with which Jean devoured the food. It presented an opportunity to explain to the nurse with a rhetorical question:

"If you take a child from a safe and loving environment and try to feed it, would it not be frightened, stressed and unwilling to accept food from a stranger?"

Five days later I was invited to the ward office to be informed by the attending doctor that there was nothing further that could be done for Jean and it was decided that she should be transferred to the geriatric ward. However, I was no longer willing to accept any further separation or loss of control and insisted on having her back home with me. My insistent demand was passed up the chain to the senior doctor in charge. After a short debate it was agreed that it was in the best interests of both of us that Jean should be cared for at home in her final days.

Arrangements were made by the hospital authorities for a rapid response team of nurses to liaise with the District Nurse in providing urgent medical home treatment as required. The lady Psychologist was contacted to offer counselling support should I require it. By the close of the month her condition had deteriorated to a state where a Community Macmillan Nurse was contacted to liaise with the doctor with reference to palliative care for Jean. Though I agreed to make contact if and when I required a visit from a palliative care team, one of their nurses visited us and I assured her I was coping fine.

One evening in July, Jean began to drift in and out of consciousness, she was very clammy and her hair was streaked with perspiration. When I failed to wake her I sought assistance from a neighbour living opposite. Although my neighbour Pamela was past retirement age, she continued to work as a Matron in a local senior's Retirement Home. Pamela was of the 'old school' of nursing; it was a vocation of love and compassion that kept her working past seventy. She agreed to sit with Jean while I requested a home visit by a doctor from the nearby surgery, a three-minute walk away. I returned home to await the arrival of the promised doctor. He arrived with his case: "Is she dying?" In response to my; "Yes," he replied:

"Well at least she's not in pain." It was time to keep control of my emotions:

"Of course she's not, she's unconscious." His parting shot as he turned to make his exit was:

"Well there's nothing I can do here."

Much later I likened the episode to Colleen, to that of the fellow who enquired of his friend why he looked so depressed. When he learned his friend had been told he had six months to live, he said: "Cheer up it'll soon pass."

Later in the evening I phoned the surgery again to request a further visit by a different doctor. It was with some relief that I greeted the young doctor who I had felt at ease and confident with from the first time we met at the start of Jean's home care. He examined her, took her temperature and arranged for regular visits during the night by the District Nurse. With a degree of compassion he helped to prepare me for the worst by suggesting that I not sit holding Jean's hand overnight:

"They tend to slip away when one goes to the bathroom or to make a drink."

As I held her hand and mopped her brow, I told her:

"It's alright to let go sweetheart if you wish, I'll be OK."

She survived the night and on the morrow consideration was given to administering oral morphine. That proved impractical and Fentanyl patches were substituted in their stead. Still the diary entries persisted in referring to my refusal to accept help. An entry beneath such a refusal reads:

"26/7/03 Paddy caring for Jean and well understands she is dying."

Further entries state that the morphine patches appear to be controlling the pain; that I was changing the patches on schedule; and I was happy that the pain was well controlled. By early August it is noted that I felt that there was very little pain and that I had resorted to using the patches only at night. An entry by one nurse in mid-September I interpreted as a show of displeasure with my decision

"Mr Rice decided to stop the Fentanyl patches as he feels Jean is not in pain."

By the close of the month the entries appeared more agreeable:

"Paddy feels Jean is no longer in pain and has discontinued Fentanyl." The October and November entries are more in tune with my actions: "Jean appears comfortable," and "Pain controlled."

Our neighbour Pamela, kept an unobtrusive eye on us and offered a welcome supply of variety packs of Ensure 'Plus' drinks as a gift. They undoubtedly contributed in some degree to the improvement in Jean's condition.

The complete picture of the Alzheimer's jigsaw puzzle began to emerge as the final pieces quickly fitted into place. By November her Handling Risk Assessment was reduced from a 'plus High Risk' to 'Medium Risk.' By

December I made an impulsive decision that was to change our future lives for the better. It was the afternoon of Christmas day; Jean was laid on the bed and we were alone. As I watched from an upstairs bedroom window a small boy riding his new bike, memories of Christmases past came flooding back. I dashed downstairs; I needed to escape. For the first time since I had brought her home I proceeded to dress Jean, lift her into her wheelchair and wrapping her up in blankets I took her out for a stroll. Along the three and a half mile journey I supported her head with one hand as we watched the Christmas lights and displays on the houses. That was the beginning of a new daily routine, plus a twice-weekly car ride to the supermarket and local shops where she had spent many years doing the weekly shopping. No longer was she to be kept from the gaze of the general public. It was with a sense of pride and honour that I accompanied her everywhere; to the bank, shops, the dentist for my check-up and to visit our daughter. When people tended to look the other way I reassured Jean:

"It's OK sweetheart, we can go anywhere because we're invisible."

People came to know and accept us. One lady at the supermarket, Vivian, became a friend and always rushed to make a fuss of Jean. It was plain to see the joy in Jean's eyes as Vivian held her hand as she spoke to her. There was no doubt in my mind that in another time the two could well have been close friends. It was also at this juncture that I had to learn the use of the hoist to transfer her safely from bed to commode and wheelchair. She had regained her natural weight of about eight stone (112lbs). The final entry in the medical diary of some twenty-eight double-sided pages of A4 was made in early May of 2004, (more than a year on) the district nurse and staff had completed their roles.

My learning was far from complete; there was still a considerable way to go with reference to her physical health. Her mental state was my primary concern and with that catered for, her physical condition was better managed. With a healthy diet, proper hygiene, exercise and with the tender loving care one would lavish on their baby, she blossomed. Her limbs required daily exercise. The hinge joints of her arms and legs I gently but slowly flexed and extended a predetermined number of times. The rotary joints of her hips, shoulder and ankles required very slow and easy movement. Her injured right hand I treated each morning during her ablutions by massaging it in a basin of warm water. Over time the best I managed to open her hand and extend the fingers was three-quarters of the way. The use of a washable pair of handgrips successfully served to improve her grip and strengthened her wrists. I had manufactured three pairs of these washable handgrips on our sewing machine. With the use of strips of crepe bandage sewed on each side and turned inside out, I had created pockets then squeezed a bathroom sponge into each pocket and sewed the ends together. The skills gained as a ten year old in the sewing machine room at Artane Industrial School came to the fore. A deep scar on Jean's left heel remained the only reminder of the dreadful pressure sores she had endured. My work on her ankles to reduce the swelling was rewarded, when for the first time in two years it was possible for Jean to wear her nice leather boots when taken out and about.

In the summer of 2004 I had a request from the lady Psychologist who had been monitoring Jean's condition prior to her expected demise. Her expression on seeing the transformation in the patient's health told its own tale. Here was a doctor that was about to leave the National Health Service but still had a passion to learn how and why Jean's condition had improved. In previous years we had discussed the background of my formative years that laid the foundations for who I had become. As she bade farewell I was touched by her parting compliment:

"It has been an honour to have met you." When she continued: "Have you ever wondered what the outcome might have been if you had the opportunity of a university education?" I had a ready story:

"In my younger days the unemployed reported to the Labour Exchange to seek work and collect their dole money. There was one man desperate to accept any work on offer. The only unfilled post was for a lavatory attendant. He failed to get the job because he was unable to distinguish between the words 'vacant' and 'engaged'; he could neither read nor write. He searched his pockets as he exited the building but he had run out of cigarettes. He had walked a few blocks before he found a shop and the seed of an idea was planted in his mind. From his weekly dole payments he religiously saved a little and from the savings he purchased a supply of cigarettes and matches to sell by the entrance to the Labour Exchange. The venture proved successful enough for him to lease a nearby property and start his own retail business. The business thrived over the years resulting in expansion to a chain of stores. His most trusted employee and friend was his accountant. One day his friend approached him to sign a cheque, a problem he always avoided by delegating the responsibility to his friend. But when he was informed of the bank's insistence that his countersignature was required for the large sum involved, he was forced to confide his secret to his friend about his inability to read or write. The accountant put the question; "Imagine what you could have achieved had you been able to read and write?" The simple answer; "A lavatory cleaner!"

As the days rolled into months I settled into a daily routine of rising at 04.40hrs to complete a morning run followed by a shower and breakfast. Between 06.00hrs and 06.30hrs I would strip Jean and place her on the commode and wheel her into the bathroom. Barefooted and in my underwear, I moved her close to the washbasin; lowered one arm of the commode and rested my foot on the commode with my leg behind her back. I held her head in my left arm against my chest while I brushed her teeth. In the beginning she kept biting the toothbrush, and then swallowed the toothpaste. This resulted in her vomiting back up her breakfast. That problem was resolved by first offering her a glass or two of water which she thirstily drank. Over time and with patience I managed to have her rinse and spit out after the first brush, then applied the paste; brushed and rinsed again. Finally I brushed her gums and she liked her tongue brushed then rinsed her mouth. With both arms of the commode lowered I removed the potty and wheeled her under the shower. When washed and dried I transferred her to the bed and used baby powder and cream prior to dressing her for breakfast. Like a child she grasped at my clothing, my hands or the towel whilst drying and dressing her.

For as long as I have known Jean I was of the opinion that she never ate a healthy diet; only picking at food and surviving mostly on snacks, biscuits and tea plus anything sweet. She took readily to the food I initially prepared:

Breakfast: One whole Weetabix with a little sugar and warm milk followed with a drink from a wide rimmed glass of Nestles Build-up (they came in a choice of flavours) in warm milk with a teaspoon of honey. Later I replaced the Weetabix with a variety pack of children's porridge (Oats So Simple).

Lunch: Potatoes, carrots, parsnips and broccoli including the meat of the day, or a piece of my omelette (made with tomato, cheese, and ham) all finely chopped and mashed, and then mixed in a bowl with a different soup every day. It amounted to about half a pint of stew. Two biscuits washed down with a drink, usually cranberry juice with a dash of Lactulose.

Evening meal: Banana finely mashed with a spoonful of honey and heated in a microwave oven; a yogurt and chocolate biscuits; washed down with Blackcurrant juice containing a dash of Lactulose.

With her weight restored and daily massages she was once again capable of supporting her head as normal. This added to the simple pleasures of our
outings to the supermarket, shops and especially our daily walks. With regular stops by an infant school playground where it was fascinating to watch as the children rushed to meet us by the wire fence. Their uninhibited curiosity was refreshing; so many questions;

"Can she talk? How does she eat? How does she clean her teeth?" "What happened to her?"

I explained: "Sometimes when your grandma, granddad or even your parents become very old, they forget things, even how to talk. If that should happens, the thing they would most want you to do is to give them lots of hugs and kisses and tell them how much you love them." One little girl told me: "I think you're very nice."

Jean and I ready for a day out and are great grand daughter Ellie

Enjoying a day out shopping

Jean looked alert as her eyes watched each of the children. Following our walk I would lay her down for an afternoon nap and often on completion of my household chores I would lay beside her. I would place her good hand around my bare back and feel her caress, whilst I held her in my arms with her head on my chest. Soon we would both be sound asleep.

Kept busy with every day tasks our precious moments of time together sped too fast. Prior to taking her to town I paid special attention to her appearance. We visited our eldest granddaughter Keri, a professional hairdresser, who attend to her hair. During the winter I arranged a home visit by a hairdresser. From a wide selection of jewellery I alternated matching earrings, necklaces and arm bangles for each of our outings. Lipstick had to be applied with care as she opened her mouth and attempted to eat it. Her summer dresses and skirts required altering as she gained weight and by the end of summer she looked tanned and healthy. We had spent much of our time outdoors wheeling her chair out on the veranda to serve her meals and to relax in the sun.

During the winter months we were both fortunate to have avoided catching colds. It was not a time to remain indoors. On dry days I wrapped her up well in a blanket and a fur hat and took a brisk walk. Her change of clothing for bedtime and morning were placed on a bedside radiator for warmth prior to dressing, plus she wore thick bed socks and a water bottle provided additional warmth. With the change of seasons she went from strength to strength though she uttered only the very rare word 'yes'. Communication was through kisses; a yes when she returned my kiss and no when she was unresponsive. On occasions she would struggle to raise her left hand to her face but never got past her chest. It was a signal that her nose, chin or lip itched. The use of a cotton bud helped to clean out her nostrils and surplus wax from her ears. In addition I organised regular home dental check-ups and treatments.

It is now strange to reflect that although we were well into 2005 it was not until the month of September that I realised we were approaching our 50th wedding anniversary. We were invited to our daughter's house for lunch to celebrate our special day. The years seemed to have passed all too soon and even then I failed to comprehend how such a very special girl had given me her unconditional love. I made a special effort to have her look her best for lunch. With a matching necklace, earrings and ring she looked lovely. Once seated in the wheelchair I went through the same routine of fastening the belt about her waist, raising the arm rests, placing her feet on the footrests. As I knelt down on one knee to strap her legs to the chair, I looked up:

"Today fifty years ago, this very day you took on this stray and married me, would you do it all over again and marry me?"

Our 50th Wedding Anniversary

I never anticipated a verbal reply, just to read her eyes but as I was about to embrace her, her face filled with emotion as she looked at me. Her mouth opened and struggled as she uttered a strangled "Yes." That was a moment in time that will last forever. We arrived at our daughter's house for a special lunch; just the three of us. I expected a quiet afternoon meal but as soon as we entered her sitting room a crowd appeared letting off streamers and offering congratulations. There was our son with his three daughters and his two sons, plus his two granddaughters. In addition there were our daughter's children; two girls, two boys and her granddaughter. Our grown-up grandchildren had also brought friends. They had made it into a truly memorable occasion.

The weeks turned into months and in no time we had entered a new year. The overwhelming power of love and the grinding hurt that accompanied it made the bitter sweet days of caring all the more palpable. Comprehension of this illness was as elusive as ever. Just when I learned something new I soon discovered how much more there was to learn. Though I had learned to always expect the unexpected I was still unprepared when it happened.

It was almost three years to the day since she first came home, when I woke her to take her for a walk. Her body went into a spasm or seizure; her eyes stared in fright as she bled from her mouth after biting her tongue. Not for the first time she was rushed to the hospital where I was refused entry to the treatment room. Once again I requested that she be returned home as soon as possible. It was late in the evening of the same day before she returned wearing a hospital gown that tied at the back. The clothing she had worn was returned in a plastic bag, they were of no further use. They had been cut off in the emergency.

As on previous occasions she recovered quickly and was physically healthy and the only indicators of further deterioration were longer periods of sleep during the day. By mid-2006 I had started giving her evening drink from a baby bottle and can recall a picture of her mouth and chin covered in chocolate. She looked the picture of contentment as she bit on the teat of the bottle and blew bubbles. We developed good communication skills by holding hands and looking into to each other's eyes as I spoke. It was possible to observe her eyes move back and forth to the right and the change in facial expressions. It tugged at my heartstrings to see her face prior to a meal; anxious to be fed but unable to cry out, then relaxed as she ate. At no stage did I ever consider including tea or coffee in her diet, it just never occurred to me.

There was a lapse of five months before she had a second seizure and once again she was rushed to A & E. On that occasion I insisted on remaining by her side at all times. Fortunately the lady doctor attending to Jean permitted me to attend once I explained the importance of my presence to her recovery. I watched the monitor attached to Jean as the line jumped up sharp then to a flat line, then up and down erratically. As she lay unconscious I talked to her all the while about the grandchildren by name; painting a picture of them playing in the orchard or by the river. I talked of Vicky the youngest girl with her pet sheep 'Pixie'.

Colleen holding her grand daughter Ellie and Jean

"Don't you worry about them they're having fun, I'll keep an eye on them, and you just enjoy a well deserved rest."

The young lady doctor was very helpful and explained that Jean could have another mini stroke any time triggered from her brain. When asked if I wished her to be kept in hospital; there was only one answer and four hours later she was home.

Time seemed to fly as we celebrated

another anniversary; 51 years of marriage followed less than two weeks later by our birthdays, Jean now 72 and me 75. Those extra years were gifts way beyond my wildest expectations.

The next seizure struck suddenly in late November as she slept in her chair after lunch. I transferred her to the bed, turned her on her side and wiped froth from her lips. When Jean went limp I called an ambulance and as usual insisted on staying with her all the while until her recovery. By the time we arrived home she appeared fine. The fits were frightening and fearful (the unknown) to both of us. To gain control and allay my fears I needed to obtain a better understanding of fits. Two days later her doctor visited and checked Jean's heart and blood pressure and found them fine. An appointment at the hospital was arranged to discover the source of the fits/seizures/mini strokes. In the meantime Jean recovered so well that some weeks later after her lunch, I said: "You know I'll still have to keep fit to be able to lift you when I'm 95?" I was dumb struck to hear "Yes"! I could not stop laughing which brought a chuckle from her.

Try as I might I never found the right buttons to press for a 'yes'. Though, I did get the very occasional 'yes' at the most unexpected times. All the while I attended to her needs I talked: "I'm your servant, what would Madam like for tea? You know you are my boss?" "Yes." Strange, why could I not get answers to more important questions?

A letter arrived from the hospital addressed

to Jean advising that an EEG appointment had been arranged for her on the 3rd January 2007. She was asked to complete a form of consent to have a video recording taken of the EEG investigation and to bring the consent form and letter when she attended. This is a Health Service that has spent a fortune on state of the art computers and yet appeared not to have recorded Jean's condition. I looked forward to the EEG tests in the hope of acquiring a better insight to her brain's function. When we arrived at the hospital for the EEG tests the doctor was surprised to find Jean in a wheelchair: "Can she feed herself?" Not for the first time I had to explain that she could neither move nor speak. Electrodes were placed about her head and hands. The tests took about an hour during which she drifted off to sleep.

The results of the tests I received a week later: Consultant's Opinion: Her EEG initially contains predominantly theta activity but as she becomes drowsy large amounts of delta activity appear. When she is alert, the delta inhibits and is replaced by faster frequencies. There are some left-sided sharp waves seen predominantly from posterior central, but sometimes from temporal regions.

The slow dominant frequency is reflecting abnormal cortical function, compatible with her known Alzheimer's Disease but there do appear to be some probably epileptiform transients coming from the left hemisphere, so this area is potentially epileptogenic. She concludes: probably Epilepsy.

She also suggested a referral to a stroke clinic for advice and suggested medication or treatment for when fits occur. The recommended medication was Diazepam Rectitude to be administered when a fit occurred.

It was left to me to arrange the Stroke Clinic appointment, which I considered urgent. Using the phone number provided by our doctor I sought to arrange an appointment straightaway. I provided all the details about my wife, and was asked:

"Does your wife know you are asking for this appointment?"

"I don't think so!" When asked which hospital I would like the appointment at I requested our local hospital.

"Sorry that's not in the loop system yet, you will have to phone the Booking Centre."

I tried phoning the Booking Centre, but got no answer, it must have been too early at 08.30hrs. Between 09.20 and 11.15hrs I kept phoning the hospital Booking Centre; each time I was put on hold, and then was told, I was 9th in line, then 7th and other times the number was engaged. After lunch I decided to lift Jean into the car and drive to the hospital. At reception I asked for the Booking Centre and made our way in that direction: "You can't go in there," the receptionist told me.

"Try stopping me, I wish to give that faceless person who kept repeating; 'you're on hold and are 9th in line etc' a piece of my mind."

"Please I'll phone the boss of the Centre and explain your problem." Surprise, she could not get through either and was put on hold! At last she understood my point and entered the centre. On her return she handed me the phone saying that the boss wished to speak to me.

"I'm sorry for what you have been through; I can arrange an appointment for your wife in February."

"I'm sorry too but that's not good enough considering my wife's condition."

"Well, give me a moment (a short pause) it normally takes eleven weeks for an appointment; however I can offer you the 30th January." "That's good, thank you."

An hour spent with the Clinician at the Stroke Clinic failed to conclude whether she had mini strokes, fits or seizures. His suggestion was the use of Junior Aspirin to thin the blood in case they were caused by small blood clots. It came as a surprise to him to learn that I cared for all Jean's needs on my own. He further questioned and recorded each of my daily activities including the food and drink I fed her, on which he remarked that it was no wonder she looked so well. I never did give her Aspirin because of the uncertainty as to the causes of the seizures. The Clinician neither agreed nor disagreed with the possibility of shock being a trigger by suddenly being awoken from a bad dream. Jean did sleep a lot and on those occasions a great fear was etched on her face and in her eyes.

Three months later she had another seizure and this time I administered the Diazepam and waited ten minutes while I cleaned her mouth. She was blue; her body limp and she had trouble breathing. Once again we rushed to hospital where she had a blood test, an x-ray and an ECG. I remained present with her throughout. That was a long day as the incident started at 09.30hrs and we arrived home at almost 16.00hrs. It meant that I had not eaten or drunk for fourteen hours but I was relieved to have Jean home.

Had I been told that Jean would have survived four years after her removal from the Nursing Home I would not have believed it and yet she passed the four year mark. To not have accepted in equal measure the negatives and positives of daily life would have been to deny the rewards of time. Jean must have been a very quiet child, which in turn contributed even more to the pleasure I derived from being with her. In addition to the usual daily drinks I found a fruit juice she thrived on; Solevita Multivitamin Nectar. As the days passed into months I became aware of our precious time drifting away. The power of overflowing love fuelled my daily efforts and the passage of time. Our fifty-second wedding anniversary was another human time marker reached along with our birthdays her's of 73 and mine of 76 on consecutive days. The fact that there was no recurrence of seizures/fits in nine months only raised my sense in expecting the unexpected. One lesson I learned was; when I thought things could not get worse, they did and when I thought I had reached the bottom, I had not. The answer was to look on the bright side of life and laugh.

The most important consideration I took on board in my caring for Jean was her emotions. She could feel pain, sadness, happiness, and a loving touch. When starved of these: stress, depression, aggression and the loss of the will to live sets in. She had been there. Daily I wrestled with the questions:

"What must be going on in her mind? How would I feel in her situation with a short-term memory? Does she feel lonely?" My only conclusion was to treat her, as I would wish to be treated in the hope of banishing her fears.

When I hoisted her from her bed to the chair for a meal she started to act like an impatient child to eat her meals and when I attempted to comfort her with a kiss she opened her mouth! Caught between laughing and crying, I then realised I had a warm loving child in my care. How few were as blessed as I? Patience was one of the many virtues I attained along the journey and by entering her world our hearts beat as one, as I kept assuring her of my happiness in being with her. She began to sleep longer and would often wake up to see me sat by her bed and close her eyes again. Nine months had elapsed since her last seizure and she looked so very well. It would be of great benefit to others if I could discover the reasons she was doing so well. I asked myself: was it the drinks? No tea or coffee? Could it be due to the absence of medication? In spite of her healthy appearance by late October I detected a slow fading of the love light in her eyes. There were periods of blankness followed by periods of clear recognition. Over the years I learned to accept the signs as a forewarning of things to come. It was also an urgent signal to cherish every last ray of love light while it showed. The warnings of time running out did not go unnoticed. In early November Jean ate her lunch within half an hour with her eyes closed. I had to wake her up for her drink. Being responsible for a fellow human being was an awesome responsibility and a very great privilege, all the more so when it is one's soul mate.

Unknowingly we were both in tune with one another's thoughts as I pleaded with her to respond to my questions with a yes or no by nodding her head or with the blink of an eye:

"When you respond to my kiss, I take it as a 'yes' and when you don't, it's a 'no.' You were sent to help me and now your work is done; you made me whole for the first time in my life. It would be wonderful if it were possible to transplant brains then you could have mine. There could be no better end to my life, knowing that you could once again enjoy life with our son and daughter and all the grandchildren. Do you love me?" A barely audible whispered 'Yes' came as a surprise, but made for a very special moment in time.

When I reflected on how I had cared for Jean during her time in hospital and the Nursing Home I became aware of the significance of being in our separate worlds. I was upset at being parted whilst she was confused and lost. Once we were reunited I entered her world and began to remove the underlying causes of depression, agitation and anxiety. Those causes had in turn led to a loss of appetite, weight loss, pressure sores and other health problems. The best medication was unconditional loving care.

Tuesday evening, 27th November 2007 was like any other, I had washed and changed Jean's pad and left her lying on her side facing towards me. I proceeded to the bathroom to empty the basin of water into the toilet, an action that took less than thirty seconds. When I returned Jean lay on the floor in a pool of blood. She had slid from the bed and fallen head first on to the wooden tiled floor. In view of her inability to move anything except her left arm, I can only assume she must have had some sort of spasm. Her inability to break her fall meant that she took the full force of the fall on her face and hand.

It had become routine by then to inform both our daughter and son of the situation and we met at the hospital. There I went though the same fight to remain with Jean at all times. Finally I succeeded in getting the message across and they were thankful for my presence whilst treating her. Jean had suffered a busted nose, chipped tooth, split lip and it was suspected a facial fracture. A young Asian lady doctor attending to Jean looked wide-eyed upon learning that I had been caring for my wife alone at home for the past four years and eight months:

"Where do you come from? Forgive me for asking but I understand that people here place family members in Nursing Homes when they become too ill to care for."

"Who I am does not matter; she is my wife, my life."

I had been up at 04.40hrs and by the time I had left the hospital it was past midnight. By Wednesday I was in no mood to eat, sleep or drink, that was until our daughter visited her Mom in the hospital and helped feed her lunch. Arrangements were made to return Jean to my care at home the following afternoon. Her eyes were almost closed from the swelling and so a nurse was arranged to visit us at home in the mornings and evenings to administer eye drops. Once again I encountered the unexpected. Within days even the nurses found it remarkable that both Jean's eyes were wide open; the swelling was considerably reduced and replaced by bright yellow marks down to her chest. Best of all she was eating and drinking well. Two days later the only meal Jean ate was breakfast. She slept late into the afternoon. Her breathing was so faint I could scarcely hear it. Her hands were clammy and limp. I raised her eyelid to reveal a blank stare. Late at night she awoke and began with a yawn. Though her pulse returned stronger she still refused to eat but did accept a drink from her bottle then drifted back to sleep. My sleep was late and restless. At five o'clock in the morning Jean awoke to accept some painkilling medication then resumed her sleep. Breakfast was late and she then slept until lunchtime. She looked refreshed and appeared to be making a full recovery. The nurses had finalised the daily eye treatment and once again we were on our own and settled back into our daily routine, except that she slept for longer periods.

On the 4th December 2007 I took Jean for a pre-arranged appointment at the Facial Fracture Clinic. From the time I lifted her into the car she slept with her mouth open and snored. Prior to our arrival I telephoned the clinic to inform them that I would remain in attendance at all times. It appeared that they already aware of my dogmatic ways!

I held Jean's head while a nurse raised her upper lip to allow the doctor to insert a stitch in her gum. A further small stitch was inserted in her upper lip. Within eight days of her fall all the swelling on Jean's face had disappeared but the evidence of the fall remained in the red marks and yellow stains. In the days that followed a lot more time and patience was devoted to feeding and washing her. Jean's recovery appeared to be remarkably rapid and I faithfully expected that within a week or two she would be returned to full health.

Saturday, 8th December started out like any other day. I had washed, changed and given Jean her breakfast; I then laid her down on her right side (facing a wall) to sleep. At 11.30 I had prepared her lunch and proceeded to transfer her to her chair for lunch. I was frightened to find her pillow was covered in blood from a nosebleed. I quickly transferred Jean from the bed to the chair, cleaned her up and tried to stem the flow of blood. When my attempts were unsuccessful I contacted the duty nurse who was also unable to stop the bleeding. Once again an ambulance rushed Jean to hospital and I contacted our daughter to meet us there. Colleen was waiting when we arrived at A & E. It was midday and we were held waiting in a queue with the ambulance crew in attendance. After almost half an hour of impatient waiting I brushed aside protests as I entered the doctor's area. During the disturbance I managed to catch the attention of the lady doctor that had treated Jean almost a year earlier. Her immediate reaction was to instruct that Jean be urgently wheeled to a treatment enclosure. After a number of attempts the doctor failed to staunch the blood flow. This young lady was totally focused on treating Jean and urgently sought advice about having Jean placed under Anaesthetic but was advised that she was unlikely to survive it. The doctor then attempted to arrange to have Jean moved to a specialist unit at another hospital some forty minutes drive away. Once again she was thwarted by the suggestion that Jean might not survive the journey. The doctor was clearly agitated and frustrated with the lack of progress she was having. She succeeded in convincing a specialist from the other hospital to travel to attend to Jean. It was late afternoon by the time the specialist arrived to 'pack' Jean's nostril. Both Colleen and I witnessed the lady doctor's extreme displeasure at the lack of urgency displayed in the treatment of Jean. The hours rolled by as we waited to see Jean safely bedded. Midnight approached and I asked a staff member what the hold-up was. We were informed that once the 'paperwork was complete' she would be assigned a bed in the admittance ward. The poor tired soul sank into a deep sleep again, deeper than before, in the mixed sex ward by the time we both left the building to make our way home in the early hours of Sunday morning.

Bedraggled and tired due to a lack of sleep and food I moved as if in a dream, aware only of some events unfolding about me. I recall vaguely spending most of Sunday at the hospital with both our son and daughter, and a period when all the grandchildren and their partners stood around Jean's bed. She lay still with a drip attached and oxygen mask; her breathing was laboured. The messages from the doctors were conflicting. Firstly I was invited to a room to speak to a foreign doctor of Middle Eastern origins, who informed me of Jean's condition; leaving me with little hope. My mind was only partly open to his words; I was already aware of what was happening. Colleen came away at the end of the day telling me that the English doctor told her that Jean could come home on the Tuesday, because he knew that I wanted her home, even if it was only for her to die in her own bed. Day and night became a seamless blur. I recall cleaning Jean's mouth with a moist sponge. As I held her clammy limp hand I could no longer see the love light shining in her eyes, it had vanished without warning, and died. She was present in body but I sensed her mind was gone. Late on Monday Colleen informed me that the doctor had changed his mind and said that her Mom was too weak to be returned home in the morning. As we departed the hospital Colleen still held faith in her Mom's ability to once again recover:

"Dad she pulled through so many times before, she'll do it again." My purpose in life was gone from me; I felt numb:

"I'm sorry sweetheart this is the end, there is no coming back."

The following twenty-four hours I moved as though in a trance, hoping and praying that what I felt was not happening. Our son and daughter alternated their presence with their Mom through to the early hours of Wednesday. It was almost five in the morning and Colleen had scarcely gotten home when she received a phone call. I was preparing to visit the hospital when the telephone rang. I froze in expectation of the worst. The tearful, childlike broken voice of Colleen pleaded with just three words;

"Dad, Mom's gone." Stunned, I fail to recollect my response. On exiting the house, there waiting to drive me to the hospital was our youngest granddaughter, Vicky. At seventeen she had suddenly grown into a young woman to the surprise of both her Mother and I. Her eyes puffed up from crying she proved to be a tower of strength as she calmly offered support as she drove to the hospital. It was hard to accept that Jean had passed away; her body was still warm and damp. With a final kiss I thought; my life and light were within thee, the pulse of my heart had stopped.

My heart ached for our son, daughter and all of their children; they had their own grief to bear. Our son had his work teaching children with severe and multiple disabilities during these days in addition to supporting his family. Our daughter was concerned about my welfare. Later I learned from him that she was worried that I would 'fall apart' as I did years earlier when our youngest child was killed. He rightly assured her that I would be all right. Nonetheless she was there to support me. Her husband returned from his work abroad, to comfort her in her time of need. He also learned that his Mother had only months to live. She passed away just weeks after Jean.

Many are the moments I reflect on our early meeting when I feared telling Jean my shameful secret about my childhood, expecting her to distance herself from me.

"Did you not have anyone in your childhood?" She thought it sad:

"No but I'm lucky I'll never know, nor can I remotely imagine the pain and hurt there must be at the loss of a Mom or Dad." Now that I have supped the bittersweet taste of love and loss, I thank God that I dared to dream and tirelessly strived to make that dream a reality.

About the Author

For his first sixteen years he had never known family life nor learned to trust anyone in times of need. All his childhood years were spent in the Irish Industrial School system. By appearing at Dublin DC as a two year old charged with `receiving alms' he was criminalised. Judge Cussen sentenced him to be detained in all boys' institutions until aged sixteen.

Thus, he joined the ranks of the ready free supply of child labour available to the religious orders that operated these `schools'. To sever all contact with family members it was decided that he not be addressed by his correct first name for the duration of his sentence.

On his release he was emotionally barren, developmentally stunted and uneducated. The absence of love and nurture in his make-up was compensated by his natural survival instincts.

He left Ireland at seventeen without regrets, to join the British Forces. His leave times were spent in bed and breakfast lodgings throughout the UK. On one such visit to Co. Durham he was smitten by a teenage factory girl, whom he asked to marry. He wasn't easily put off by her first refusal and three years later they were married.

Her unconditional love not only proved his

salvation, but was a powerful motivator to pursue and achieve what appeared impossible life goals. His early life's experiences fuelled his ability to singularly take on the roll of carer when his wife could no longer move or speak due to Alzheimer's.

He ignored the professional advice that `it is impossible for one person to care for a patient in the end stage of Alzheimer's.' After almost five years of caring 24/7 365, he felt privileged to have gained a deep understanding of this mind stealing illness that he strongly wishes to widely share.

Lightning Source UK Ltd.
Milton Keynes UK
08 December 2009

147236UK00001B/3/P